Quest of the Golden Stairs

(1927)

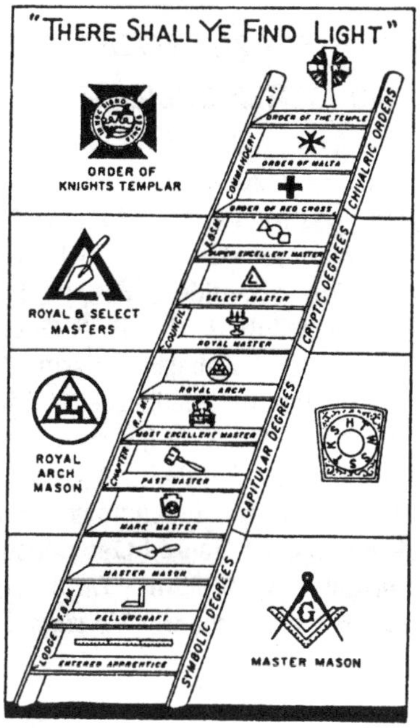

Arthur Edward Waite

ISBN 0-7661-0748-5

Contents

The Quest of the Golden Stairs

I

THE COURT OF STARS

A Diadem in Faërie

"There is a Crown suspended in Faërie, shining on a far height," said the BOOK OF THE VOICES OF FAËRIE, which is called THE SWORN BOOK. But that which must be done to win it is not declared in words, save only in hidden places. A Faërie above the sea and a Faërie also beneath, a Faërie under the earth, but also in woods and forests, and all the open ways: the wonders of these are with us. But of Faërie over the hills there is nothing told in the histories: yet is it highest of all. "I am he who returns therefrom as a bearer of many tidings," said one of the Wise Masters who spoke in the leaves of the Book. "There is a story here concerning the Crown of Faërie, and this I shall tell you because it is faithful witness, full of truth in the art. It was given me by a Provost of the Palaceon a May-Day in the morning, at the head of a green lane beyond the violet hills." If you had been there, you would know that it is beautiful.

"On that other side of the world which is not reached by walking, it befell on a day," said he who was a Prudent Master, "that all the Kings were old, and hence when each in his turn should fall asleep in lavender, the Thrones of Faërie might be vacant. It came about therefore that, seeing its Law of Succession is other than rules on earth, the peoples of Faërie grew weary of Kings without end —Kings of the precincts and byways, Kings of the four quarters, signs and decanates of Faërie, of cities which shine in moonlight, cities above and below, and great cities in the sea. So they put up their petition to the Twelve Houses of Heaven, a great Court of Stars, praying for one King who should rule over all Faërie, even all Kings therein, in the power and glory of wisdom.

Souls crying out in Faërie

"Sing me your songs, ye birds, wild white Swans of Faërie: I am a Knight of the Swan; and I, who carried the petition, testify that the Court of Stars received the prayer with favour. On a hill-top in Faërie which looks over land and sea, and from which it may happen at times that a Golden Staircase winds up to the Court of Stars and its Holy Houses, they raised a jewelled throne. Moreover, they placed thereon a sceptre of green malachite and suspended an emerald crown, as symbols of universal royalty. They encompassed the Throne and Insignia with great consecrations, to guard them against all comers but him whom they should choose in a due time, according to gifts of prevision in the Twelve Houses of Heaven.

Voices of the Law

"In fine, the Court of Stars made a Covenant under the Rainbow to insure the dominion of him who sat on this Throne in Faërie; and I, as the witness thereof, have descended the Golden Stairs, empowered to proclaim the tidings. I certify also that all the Kings of Faërie have fallen asleep in lavender and that the Throne of Faërie is vacant.

"Come quickly therefore, ye who are called in the heart: one shall be chosen perchance; and after royalty in Faërie he shall ascend the Golden Stairs to the Court of Stars."

Listen therefore, and hear: the Bells are ringing in Faërie

II

THE BOOK OF THE VOICES OF FAËRIE

The Master of the House stood at the door of the House in the old porch, while the stars began to kindle over the sea. It was a grey, half-ruinous building in a waste and marish chase. At the side of its stately Master stood an honourable stripling, his son and Son of the House. He was called Prince Starbeam. A ship rocked at anchor without the bay, at an arrow's flight from shore. The Master of the House was embarking on a long voyage, full of peril and venture, on a great and secret quest, to raise up the ruined fortunes of his royal race—that ancient line of Kings. A flight of broad steps led from porch to garden and on either side were time-old handrails of hammered iron. Tears stained the cheeks of Prince Starbeam as the Master kissed his son and so went forth from the mansion. The stars watched him in his passing, and those twin stars which were the boy's eyes watched him also through obscuring veils.

Fishing for Stars in the Sea

The house, which stood upon a sheer cliff, had one high turret overlooking land and sea. It was a custom of the place that a bright lamp should burn in this turret, as a warning to ships at sea, for between the cliffs there was a bay with good anchorage. When Prince Starbeam made an end of his grieving, he climbed the spiral stairs to trim and light the lamp. It was a code of honour in the House that only the Master or his son should discharge this office. Thus had it been from the day when a light was first set up therein, and the earliest lesson learned by every heir of the House was to replenish the lamp and

The Lost Houses of Faërie

to light it. When this art had been mastered, he was put to that of reading, and when he could read there was placed before him a great and high Chronicle of the rise, race and royalty of his ancient line, its princes and valiant women, the prelates who had sprung from it, the Grand Masters in Council, its poets and men of wisdom, the deeds which they had done, the wars which some had fought in, and the Traditional Knowledge of the House. When the Son of the House had been instructed in this its history, he was given a noble book of Knightly Romances and the BOOK OF THE VOICES OF FAËRIE, including the QUEST OF THE GOLDEN STAIRS. Such was the custom of the place, and thus had it been with Prince Starbeam.

When he had lighted the lamp, on this day out of days in the year, the boy went down into the book-room and sat in the bay of the great oriel window, the tale of the Golden Stairs open on his knees—an old quarto volume in Gothic letters, with a massive cedar binding and brass clasps. However, he was not reading, for his eyes were fixed upon the sea, where a white-sailed ship was sinking slowly out of view, on the far verge in the moonlight. He was not reading, but in thought he went over the tale of hidden meanings, while the Quest of the Golden Stairs and his father's quest were wrought one into another in a waking dream of the mind. The ship had passed beyond his ken when he closed the worshipful book: then resting his elbows thereon and his chin on his hands, he began to question and plan, to weave the spells of his dreaming, half in an earnest mood, half in fancy's play, about his father's voyage and venture.

Jewels of Prophecy

"There is one straight road in Faërie, and this is the Path of the Moon; but it is seldom travelled by man. There through the lighted spaces my father's ship sails forth. He reaches lost realms of enchantment; he passes wandering isles, isles that are seen and some that are heard only—by means of their music. His shall be hills of vision and pomp of coasts unknown, beneath the sunset lights. The quest that is given him by high sea-queens is the treasure of the sea, the gold and the fine stones, all sunken freight of ships. He will gather the harvest in and return from his long voyage. He will come up the landing-steps with a heart of joy. Through the rye-field and over the path, over the purple hill, so to the Castle Hall, full of pages, squires and knights, and a dream of sweet women from Faërie. What must I do to be worthy when he builds up the House in splendour, when he sits in his chair of state and renders to man and maid according as their worth shall be ? "

Prince Starbeam leaned back in his own chair, and the moonlight cinctured his rich curls and broad white brow. " Queen of the dreams and the dreamers," he thought and cried, " Moon in the House of Beauty, is there anywhere a quest like the Quest of the Golden Stairs ? Upward and upward they wind, says the BOOK OF THE VOICES OF FAËRIE ; but who shall tell where they lead, or what is the Court of Stars ? Are they wide and bright and shining ? Do they go up to heaven, like the rainbow, and do they descend again ? Where shall I seek them ? " he asked, in commune with his own heart. " Will the books in this book-room tell me ? I will search them all to learn ; and then I will go over earth and sea, that I may find the Golden Stairs."

Moons of Paradise

The moon brightened in heaven : from silver to gold on the sea's surface turned its hallowing light. His heart swelled within him at the joy and glory of the quest. The wind rose and shrieked through corridors and galleries, where the ghosts of that old House walked and watched in the night-tide. Prince Starbeam ascended to his room and opened the lattice of a lancet window high in the western wing. Stars without number were shining over land and sea; and sea-voices came to him in the wind's pauses, as if they were music of the spheres. About

The Descent of Stars from Heaven

midnight the stars began to fall from heaven, shooting in bright meteoric arcs, and the Son of the House was wrapt away from himself, seeing the world and its splendour.

The next day, in the age-old book-room, full of muniments and archives, Prince Starbeam began his search for the Golden Stairs among illuminated manuscripts and vellum memorial scrolls. At the end of a year he had filled his head with secret writings and ciphers, with strange histories in poems, leaden and golden legends, yet of the quest he had learned nothing, though the name of the quests was legion. It was now the anniversary of that day when the Master of the House had started on his long voyage, and remembering this the eager heart of Prince Starbeam failed for a little moment.

"My father will return from radiant voyage and venture," he said, "but he will find his son idle, and my hands will be empty. I shall droop my head for shame because I have done nothing. Yet if I had found the Golden Stairs I should watch in the old porch and hail his advent proudly." He could not contain himself as he thought of the victory and green wreath of that meeting. He went forth then into the porch, and standing with outstretched hands, he saw that the night had fallen. The

Moss-covered Mountains of Faërie

moon had risen over woods and high over hills eastward. He prayed that the Queen of Quests might send him a Spirit of Quest who should lead him to the Golden Stairs. The wind from sea, which had been trumpeting about the old House, died suddenly in whispers, and there was a deep hush, as when a heart learns in the stillness. The inspiration of the young poet's voice held earth and ocean, like a Mage with lifted wand.

Who has been in the silence of Faërie, and has heard the tears of Faërie fall therein ? Who has heard the voice of its gladness shrill through the silence, like a pibroch over the hills ? But the moon has its own Faërie : who has watched in the silence when dreams come down on the sleeper from the secret heart of the moon ? There was a night of dreams for Prince Starbeam, and when silence of darkness began to stir with morning, he was going forth from the old mansion, conscious of new intimations, a great inward awakening—as if the shadows that dwelt therein had been lifted up from his heart. The grim carvings and faded tapestries of its oaken rooms ; the book-room, with its long rolls and parchments ; the rise and royalty of his race ; the ghosts which thronged the corridors : these things slipped backward—as into a far past of memory. He looked on the flashing sea, where mists folded up on its surface, and it seemed good that he should seek the Golden Stairs over that free expanse. He went up a hill of vision, the third highest point in that country, and it seemed well that he should seek them over the wide earth, through cities and solitudes. He descended that hill and went forward, as into a strange land, where shone another sun, and a deeper tincture of light fell upon weir and wold. He knew now that any path will lead him who is born to the quest. The beginning of non-beginning and end of endless : such are the quest and term. It was as if an invisible hand raised up a light to shine without and within him, and in that light he saw that he was a Son of the Quest—born and called and chosen. It was as if the BOOK OF THE VOICES OF FAËRIE were written in light about him, over all he passed and saw. On the obverse side of its cedar covers a graver's pen had emblazoned in great letters the words FAITHFUL AND TRUE ; and to Prince Starbeam, faring forward in that other light of morning which he saw for the first time

Horns of Dilemma in Faërie

with his own eyes, the attestation spoke plainly, even like records of travellers who find their own stories written in strange books. Whether he was chosen or not by the Court of Stars to fill that jewelled throne, he was called at least to the Quest. He had dwelt on the borders of Faërie through all his days and the sense of its glamour had passed through all his life; but it was rather the Golden Stairs and that which lay beyond than a glory of Kinghood in Faërie which drew his heart in longing. He travelled onward and onward, a procession of voices following. Whatever the end thereof and whether an end was reached, the joy of quest was with him, enough for an eager life—faring through days and years. So did the stars lead him, with a growing sense of guidance on his own part.

The Sensitive Life of Faërie

It is well to remember the end on the way to Faërie; it is well to forget the end in the rapture of reaching Faërie: the end may shape itself at the top of a rapture. To him who can open a door which leads within to Faërie, the end is everywhere. For the season and day at least, such a door was standing ajar in Prince Starbeam's state of vision; and when he saw once again the old, old towers of his house, a mile or more in the distance, it did not seem to him that he had lost by turning backward the true way of the quest. He was moving presently through the middle place of a woodland, where the linden whispered secrets and beneath it were sweet waters which answered in light and shade. Many secrets are held in the deep brown wells of Faërie. He came in his faring to a clear and shining pool. It must have been fed by a spring welling up from afar in the earth, for it overflowed in a little stream, which wound its way through the wood, starred on the sides with flowers, as the pool was starred also with shining water-growths. A host of red foxgloves in Faërie congregated about the marge. So gentle,

A Carpet of Dreams in Faërie

however, were the spring's forces that motion was suggested only rather than seen on the pool and a still life in the depths. A still life indeed, but the water gives up in Faërie its living things and its images, its portraits of those who are present, its pictures of absent faces. As Prince Starbeam stood and dreamed, the violet eye of heaven—reflected within the surface—assumed a deeper tinge. He lost the sense of a pool in the sky's image; he lost the sense of sky, as one who unawares looks into his own heart, and his heart shews in the silence that love is the life of quest. He was fathoming now without knowing a deep of love. A little while, and he sank on his knees by the pool, where something eternal had opened in a face of love, the face of a maiden like the world's desire for dignity and in beauty like a quest attained. It shone upon him, full of worship and sweetness, a radiant image in the waters, speaking with eyes to eyes, and as soul to soul in the silence. So were they pledged to each other in fathomless deeps of stillness.

It was thus with the Prince and his vision, as it might be, a brief contemplation. Thereafter he knew only of mists on the water at nightfall, of purple shadows veiling the pool's surface, enfolding darkness about him, and then a moon in heaven. The wood was far behind him. He raised up his face; a moon-ray fell thereon; he went up the steps of his house, under the old porch. On that same night a ship dropped anchor in the bay between the cliffs, and in that same hour the Master of the House came back after long voyage and venture for the restoration of his ancient line. Who stood in the porch to welcome, and not as if with empty hands?

The Wooings in Faërie and the end of all the Wooings

III

THE MAGIC RING

There is the very heart and the centre, which is the place of Kinghood in Faërie, the place of many Kingdoms and rulers of old therein. But there are also the realms about, those on the borders and those that are far away, so far and so haunted. They are called Faërie in the Chronicles, for all that happens therein, and all that leads therefrom, even to the heart and centre, is made in its likeness and filled with its own spirit.

The Bow of Promise in Faërie

On one of the borders of Faërie the Lord Royal of the Golden Isles ruled over a great nation, as nations are counted in Faërie. At that time when the Throne of the Kinghood was vacant, the High Court of Stars, being mindful of its Covenant, sent down a Messenger, even that Master in Chief of the Portal whose faithful testimony was recorded in the SWORN BOOK OF THE VOICES OF FAËRIE. He wore the rainbow vesture of the Covenant, and in his girdle was that Golden Key which is found—by those who are chosen—at the foot of the Rainbow. His mission, however, concerned not the Key of Faërie but the gift of a Magic Ring to the daughter of the Lord Royal, that she might overcome the weird thereof and so make ready for a Kingdom, which was other than the Golden Isles. There are rings of enchantment, rings of evil seeming and rings of false glitter; there is also the ring of not seeing, for those who go invisible; but the true jewels of Faërie are like suns shining with their own light, while the fairest gems of earth are moons at best and brightest, having only a borrowed lustre. The Magic Ring which came from the Court of Stars had the Twelve Houses of Heaven as an indrawn lustre within it and the quickening of a hidden life. It was a giver of youth and beauty to those who wore, so that time in the passing could write no record upon them, whether or not there were other forces at work which wrote on their inward side. It was known concerning this gift, of which there were older examples in the CHRONICLES OF THE COURT OF STARS and the State Papers of Faërie, that it is not in the time of possession a gift of perfect joy, and that while it may devolve on the owner to find an heir in succession, it is not transferred lightly. There are tales of old sorrow in Faërie concerning a Magic Ring. *Of the Old Drolls and the Legends*

The daughter of the Lord Royal was like the splendour and brightness of the Moon, a Diana and an Artemis for Uranian glory in vision. The names of Faërie are not the names of this world, and it is by way of substitution only that she is to be called Princess Cynthia in this poor earthly transcript. The air opens in Faërie, the air gives up visions, the air takes back and shuts down. It was after this manner, in a hidden close of the gardens about the Palace of the Isles, that the Master in Chief of the Portal came on his mission of Stars, amidst tinctured speech of sunset, tongues of purple and gold. Of the mission he spake nothing, nor yet of a vacant throne; but amidst the dyes and their music he told her how the Court of Stars, in the Twelve Houses of Heaven, had decreed a dower in their wisdom against the day of her marriage, a Ring of youth and beauty, to have and to hold henceforth, awaiting a day to come when their will should be shewn further. She standing a maid amazed, he placed the Ring on her hand, then raising the hand upwards, as one who makes an oblation, he added these worshipful words: "To the will of the Court of Stars and the ends of life in Faërie." Thereafter the air received him, as one who goes inward.

The Princess Cynthia found another refuge in the solitude of her own apartments, and—since it must be said—she sorrowed rather than rejoiced in her first possession of a gift from the Court of Stars, for there was a deep within her responding to the words of the Messenger in a voice of dole. Those who have been to the Silent City know that a hand unseen writes the great tale of silence wherever a wall is built; but that which followed this voice was the loneliest silence which ever came over a heart in the ways of Faërie. Those who have been in the City of Darkness have heard one voice in the gloom which tells the great tale of darkness. Hereof was that voice of dole. But who can be wise for the asking or wise in asking not?

The City and the Solitude

The Lord Royal of the Golden Isles was delighted beyond measure when he came to hear of the gift and the mode of its giving. He resolved that the Princess Cynthia should be wedded to one only who owned a similar talisman against the power of time. It was intolerable to suppose that a heart of endless May-time could be yoked to a heart which would be presently in winter-frost. However, he sought in vain for another person possessed of a Magic Ring; and in fine—his Council concurring—he made a proclamation through the length and breadth of his domains, offering the hand of his daughter and the heritage of his own Kingship to any suitor, whether prince or peasant, who owned or could obtain a counterpart jewel under gift from the Court of Stars. So did the Twelve Houses of Heaven work through the will of others to reach their proper ends. Proclamation was made accordingly, and it reached in time that old, old mansion in the waste and marish chase, where dwelt Prince

Starbeam, and whither from voyage and venture returned the Master of the House. Hereunto therefore is the first story concerning the Magic Ring.

Houses of Exchange in Faërie and of what may be bought and bartered

IV

THE BELOVED KINSMAN

Old as a Moon of Faërie

The Master of the House stood at the door of the House in the old porch, and the Moon loomed dimly through thin white mists, moving from a quiet sea. He received his son's glad welcome with a failing heart, for the quest itself had failed. Within the measures of his own apprehension, it had fallen to pieces utterly; and the fortunes of the House seemed lost. The fabled treasures had passed in a cloud of dream. There was a Bright Land lying under a Bright Sky where once his sires had dwelt, according to the Legends of the House, and had reigned as lords therein. He had followed a false light, hoping to return thither, and had gone over earth and sea; but such a bourne of quest is sought in another manner. After all, the Earthly Paradise is not exactly of earth, and the gold of Faërie is not a freight of ships, whether they sink or sail. So the night of his cloud was on him and it made a night in the House, though Prince Starbeam dwelt himself on a hidden or further side of the boding gloom, in a peculiar glory of his own. Day by day he fared to the Haunted Well, and ever that well gave up the Blessed Vision to his eyes. It was thus, as it felt to him, for the space of a single Moon, but who shall say what luminaries had waxed and waned in the mundane heaven without?

Have you walked in the gardens of Faërie, gardens far and away, a world's end of gardens? In the waste about that ancient House it is told that there was also a garden which had been ever Prince Starbeam's care; and because it was on the borders of Faërie, or because the strings of his human nature had been tuned to the strings of all those harps and viols which the blessed spirit of the world strikes in the world without, it was a place of music and beauty, life and its verdure, fragrant blossoms of life and the fruit of life everywhere. But the woods open in Faërie, and here or there on the precincts wonder is followed by wonder, moving like painted scenes. And beyond the garden was a meadow, while beyond the meadow was a forest, which was very old and of vast extent. Prince Starbeam stood in his garden, once on a day or its morning, and heard a sweet voice singing the same song, as it seemed to him, over and over. In the middle of the night after, he awoke and the same voice sounded in his own garden. He leaned through an open window and looked out over a transfigured earth; but no living being was to be seen. The next morning there was a new paradise in the garden, as if it had been created newly by the magic of that wandering voice; and though the voice itself had travelled beyond hearing its echoes and whispers breathed forth unawares from the inmost being of some of the unknown plants.

The Lifting of Voices in Faërie

It was at this time that the proclamation of the Lord Royal reached the solitary chase, and a new hope stirred in the broken Master of the House. Stars also speak and planets move in music. There were figures of the Houses of Heaven hidden in the old book-room, and at the time of Prince Starbeam's birth they had told of great things stored up for the boy. So he called the Son of his House and bade him go forth in search of a Magic Ring, that he might wed the Princess Cynthia and inherit the crown of the Golden Isles. In such manner should the Glory of the House be restored, and a path might open thereafter to the Bright Land lying under a Bright Sky. But the House of Prince Starbeam's vision shook from summit

The Stars speak in Faërie

to base as he heard the high command, and this was the first occasion on which he revealed to anyone his great secret concerning the Haunted Well, and his love of the Dream-Lady whose face shone therein. To the Master of the House it was only further proof of that which the stars had prophesied; and so when the night had fallen he took him up narrow stairways to the roof of the highest tower and shewed him the planet Jupiter shining in the mid-heaven, full of benignant auspices. In the name of those auspices, in the name of the old House and all the dereliction of its needs, he laid the quest upon him, with a solemn adjuration and under penalty of doom to come: that he should set forth presently, or two days hence, on his journey, having his face to the setting sun, because he who goes westward shall meet for a certainty with great and strange adventures. Late in its rising, a red moon soared up suddenly in the East, like a new witness in heaven. And they went down together, to wit, the father and the son. The darkness of the House received them; the cold hand of all its omens and portents was laid on the heart of Prince Starbeam: its story of dole interposed for a moment between him and the promise of the Haunted Well.

The Sale of Kingdoms in Faërie

"My Lady will be lost to me for ever," he thought, in the lone night thereafter. "What must I do? If I obey not my father, he will curse me; but if I follow his mandate and should indeed win the Princess, we shall be wretched, both of us, through all our endless days, for I have heard that she loves a Prince, and he is denied her, since he has not a Magic Ring."

Light of the distance shining, star of the days to come: the planet Jupiter, like a lord of benign countenances, shone over the old House; the Court of Stars and the Twelve Houses of Heaven pondered with smiling hearts, because of a hidden secret, and made no pause in their work of drawing gold threads together, without haste or violence.

A voice says: " God keep you at night "—when darkness falls upon Faërie. The dream in the heart of Prince Starbeam was nearer than eyelids and eyes to his Blessed Vision. Yet the stars are good watchers of secrets, and hence if he dreamed well, it was not after all too wisely. When he woke up next morning the events of the previous day were themselves for a moment no better than troubled dreams, and he went betimes through the forest to visit the Haunted Well. Who follows the track of the lizard shall come to the spring's source; but he found that the well was dry, and all that he saw was a green lizard crawling among the stones. With faculties suspended, with blank eyes fixed on the shining pebbles, he stood as a stone statue, but there was a noise in his brain like the surging of a torrent. It was a bright, bright day, running with golden hours. O tales told by the throstle and birds that chant legends: there was singing of birds everywhere; and the wind, full of scented secrets, whispered and crooned among answering leaves and dappled shadows on grasses. It might have been eventide when silence fell for a space, and then the shrill voice of a lark pealed in the empyrean, without stint in its ecstasy. There are worlds beyond wells in Faërie and wells in the world of song. A fountain deeper than these unlocked in Prince Starbeam's heart and flowed over in saving tears. So opens the heart in Faërie, and so in otherwhere.

To Lose is to Find in Faërie

Many things answer the dreamer, but there are certain pauses of moments when nothing speaks like the silence. Such silence fell with the darkness, as he turned on his homeward way, and so came to the densest part of the forest. A promise of life, a promise of joy therein stole through his heart in the stillness. He could scarcely distinguish objects a few feet in front of him; as he passed low bushes and stumps of trees, some of them wore an uncertain resemblance to human figures. When he was aware presently of an undefined object moving in the path before him, it seemed at first like an animal, and as he loved rather than feared most wild things of the woodland, he took quicker paces forward and then saw that it was a human being bending under a large burden. He remembered the Wood-Boys whom he had seen often at evening, bearing logs and peat to be stored for winter fires; but there had never been one so weighted, stumbling at every step and almost at sinking point. There is a Wheel of Fortune in Faërie which only Kindness turns: between an opening in the trees above, the planet Jupiter shone like a Court of Stars.

"Let me help you," said Prince Starbeam eagerly, as he came to the bearer's side, who lifted his eyes, shining with a strange light.

"Will you take it all from me?" the wayfarer asked faintly, and it was not with the voice of a Wood-Boy.

"Yes, all," Prince Starbeam answered. "I am strong and can carry it lightly."

"It is not mine but yours," said the other, "and I will put it so on your shoulders."

Good Deeds come Home in Faërie, World without End

Prince Starbeam received it willingly, but it seemed much heavier than any peat or faggots. He could form no idea of its nature; but when he had borne it a little distance his back and his knees were bending. He who had been liberated was also changing slowly. He walked with head erect and looked about the age of his companion. They had passed the densest growth of the forest and now emerged on a border, where over wide meads and distant melancholy marshes they saw empurpled fires still smouldering in the West. A belated level sunbeam fell upon them both for a moment, and Prince Starbeam cried out at the great transformation of the pilgrim, who now stood beside him in royal robes and invested with unearthly beauty. He wore a crown of stars and his sandals were of golden woof, wrought about with rubies which shone with dusky fire. O the charity of Faërie and the ways of the paths of loss: in that same moment the burden fell from Prince Starbeam, who rose also to his proper height, full of grace and youth. It was youth and grace of nature, but that other had the aspect of one who is commissioned from a Court of Stars. Count me the stars of Faërie, for these are a great nation, spinning their threads of gold: when will they draw together? The bright apparition drew and folded the Prince in his arms, saying: "I have put my love upon you. Love is the passport and love is the yoke in Faërie. Look therefore and see."

Prince Starbeam looked behind him, following an index hand. There was fragrance of nard and spikenard, but of the burden he saw nothing.

"It is in the heart of my beloved henceforward, to have and to hold. I have come out of the great distance for your love's sake, as a brother. Give unto me love for love."

"Till the asphodel moves the mountain," Prince Starbeam answered—then also and not previously taking the speaker in his arms. The length of the journey to Faërie is the length of a kiss too short. They kissed there in the night-light, and for a moment the Gates of Faërie opened in the lips which touched him.

The Power of a Kiss in Faërie

"The first link of the destiny. Link up your chain, my brother. By this are you signed and sealed, that none shall take or hold you, and that I shall be yours and watch."

"Leave me not yet" is Faërie, and with the breath on his mouth of that kissing Prince Starbeam said: "Be then at my side for ever, that we two may be one heart in the peace or war of the worlds."

"Nay," said the other, and in his voice there was a

tincture of sadness, or a note like the lone ocean. "At this moment must we part; but afterwards you shall know what I am, within sound of the Bells of Faërie."

"What are you? How shall I call you?"

"Look into my eyes."

They were large, grey and luminous. As the magnet draws the steel, they drew Prince Starbeam's soul in unspeakable longing. Of such is the work of a kiss: that was surely a voice only—far up in the high heaven— which said: "Prince Starbeam, Prince Starbeam: I am the Beloved Kinsman."

Alone and long in the darkness he wearied heaven with eyes. At length a clock in the distance chimed four quarters and began striking the hour. As one in a deep abstraction, Prince Starbeam counted the strokes, and at the twelfth he was standing unawares in the porch of the old House.

Betwixt the murmurs of the breeze and woods, the voice of Bells in Faërie

V

THE PARADISE OF BIRDS

The fauna and flora of Faërie speak in the eventide. You may hear in the morning also their greeting of strangers and that which, one with another, they exchange through all the hours. There is a thinner veil over its living things than over those on this earth of ours; there is a stronger chord of sympathy between them and the manifest humanities—therein and about the threshold. It is not literally that they speak human language but rather that we understand their meanings, by the help of quickened sympathy. So also the language of birds interprets itself to those who have the freedom of Faërie in the tongue native to each. It is not a secret of speech but one of understanding. This is the sense in which the tongue of men becomes the tongue of birds. "Sing me to sleep and dreams, ye white-winged Swans of Faërie: I know your word in my heart." The freedom of Faërie is kept in the heart's casket: its titles are tenderness and love; its gift is oneness with Nature, or the spirit which dwells in all. Behold, there is Kinship everywhere, and the world is growing up—man to a diviner stature and the blessed living creatures to man. O feed my lambs in Faërie; water my sheep in Faërie: pity on Kine in Faërie is pity of gold. The secret is always: Thy need is greater than mine. He that would see with his own eyes the joys of Faërie must wipe away tears from others. And this Prince Starbeam knew. He knew that the freedom of Faërie may be found in a cup of water, given in the good God's name. It is a place where God finds out His own.

Raise me the Veil of Faërie

Works of Mercy in Faërie

In the garden of Prince Starbeam, which grace of the heart and its gladness had salved from the waste chase, the life of the wood and the fell met in thicket and brake, and the winged life of air. But the birds are messengers who carry the tidings of Faërie all over the country side, and these were a wealth in the garden—wealth of plumage and wings, wealth of the world of music. For often and ever at need the youth had stood sponsor for Providence, in all the states and degrees of feathered life—those of the egg and fledgling, those of the broken wing and the victim of the hunter's shaft, those of the father of tribes and the nursing mother of babes. So did he grow in their knowledge and their love about him grew, while it seemed to him at times and seasons that they spoke a common tongue, though not with lips or bills.

On the day after his coming who was called the Beloved Kinsman, Prince Starbeam received the final commands of his father to set forth at once on the Quest of the Magic Ring. He was therefore—as it seemed to him—for a last time in his garden, thinking sadly how soon the waste might reclaim its Eden, of the weeds about the Haunted Well and the weary wilds of quest, when the heart has no share therein. A familiar dove had been missing from her home in the garden, but about noon he found her panting and travel-stained on a bed of ivy, over against the dove-cote. He lifted up his hands of healing to smooth her ruffled feathers, and gave her food and water. The day wore towards evening; the evening cooled to night; sounds of voices and music came to him from a village hard by, for now it was harvest home. A new moon of Faërie was sinking westward into the dark arms of the forest, when a large bird perched before him on an apple-tree and uttered a few silvery notes, like an elfin bell for clearness. It was a strange visitant in the garden and shone with Iris hues, as a star in the tulip shines. Prince

Starbeam stretched forth his arm, inviting it to rest thereon, but it remained amidst the red russet of the fruit, with bright eyes in the shadow, still uttering the same quick, musical sound. O the notes which are words in Faërie, and the meaning behind the words, like verses ringing in the ear. The youth heard with his ears, the youth understood in the heart. "Call me in verses of Faërie: I have come out of the great distance," the message seemed to say.

The Sunlight speaks therein

Over the hillside and hollow, to a place that is very far away; through the dusk and the dark and the daylight, over the borders of Faërie; through visions of sunrise and moonset; through gulfs of life which open in the heart of planets, he was called to a Paradise of Birds, called to the heart of Faërie. It was like a transcript from the BOOK OF THE VOICES OF FAËRIE or a summons from the Court of Stars. He approached the beautiful messenger, and a covenant was made with the eyes between the youth and the bird. He went back into the House, and his father—having heard and seen—gave thanks to the Houses of Heaven. Thereafter he arrayed his Childe, as for royal quest and venture, even a pilgrimage of stars. He looked not now as the Son of a Fallen House but Prince of the Bright Land lying under a Bright Sky, adorned with spiritual beauty. The Master covenanted to keep the lamp burning in the high turret, to warn all ships at sea. So he led his boy to the porch and left him under the porch, saying: "Farewell, and God speed: to the lead of the rainbow-bird and the prize of the Magic Ring."

But Prince Starbeam answered: "To the end of the days in Faërie, to the end of all the days," because he remembered the Kingdom and the tale of its vacant throne. He followed the low flight of the strange bird through the arches and wilds of the garden, over the beaten path which skirted the hither side of the forest;

Palaces of Flowers

and then they plunged into its depths. The bird perched on his shoulder, till the pale light of an early morning shone through the green leaves. Ye pillars of trees in Faërie, what of the path between? It led to the further borders, as darkness leads to dawn. A world of meadows stretched in the light beyond, and thereafter a white road, winding among hills, took them westward through the whole day—past hamlets, villages and country inns. There is ever a larder in Faërie and ever a flagon of wine; but, with the bird for his guide, Prince Starbeam felt neither fatigue nor hunger. There is a Bread eaten in the heart, an awakening food of life.

The stream is clear and flows, how bright and shining: it moves to its own music, a voice of many parables. They crossed such a stream in the whispering eventide. They skirted a low hill which overlooked a cloud-sea and came to a lonely house, with embattled parapet, standing among old trees on the hill-side.

The rusty key may open a house of plenty, and a wicket-gate may lead into places of mystery. They passed through such a wicket and went up a grove of oaks, where the bird broke forth in music, to which the trees made answer, with vibrant echoes shaken from innumerable leaves. It is good to be young in Faërie; to be fair in Faërie is better; but to be loving and kind in Faërie is like the Wishing-Cap of Fortunatus and the way to a Court of Stars. The heart of Prince Starbeam had opened and so had the bird's heart; thus had they found a language. Prince Starbeam knew thereby not only whither he was going but that here was the journey's end, and the Home of Birds in Faërie. For the time being at least he knew also their secret ways and their poems. His dream seemed deepening as he traversed the mighty grove and felt the cold creative wind which breathed round that storehouse of Nature. From this house come forth the birds of

Trees of Healing

Faërie and thither also they return. It had the appearance at first of an ordinary antique dwelling, but when the youth paused beneath the eaves it seemed suddenly of vast extent and height, a glory of building expanded, a castle carried onward into the great distance, with domes and pinnacles, all in the sunset after-glow. Birds of the Paradise of Faërie, birds of those garden grounds went in and out incessantly, and through the groves and the bowers, as thoughts which come and go through a man's head. But over and within the building there dwelt an invisible spirit, a sacred and quiet presence, like the nobility of an indwelling thought in a mighty cosmos.

The Flight of Birds

They crossed the threshold, so passing into a noble hall, and as this was traversed by Prince Starbeam his footsteps awoke a thousand sleeping echoes, like music and speech of music. At the further end was an archway, hung about with curtains of green samite, on which an olive-branch was embroidered, as if beyond it might be "a quiet night and a perfect end," even World's End in Faërie. Some voice beyond invited Prince Starbeam to enter, and so parting the curtains he passed to an inner chamber, where he found himself in the presence of one who had the aspect of that Knight of the Swan in the BOOK OF THE VOICES OF FAËRIE, when he descended the Golden Stairs with a Covenant from the Court of Stars. He had the aspect also of him who is true of voice in witness, and he had eyes that the heart has not fathomed, like those of the Beloved Kinsman. The bird left Prince Starbeam's shoulder and as one who at length comes home he sought the breast of his Keeper, who smoothed the rainbow feathers and passed him through an open window into a glory of gardens beyond. The bird flew quickly away in a storm of bird-music and into a strange, magnetic light, as a health of life in life. The songs of this world are shadows of songs in Faërie, and the notes which flowed through the window or poured therein were fountains in a garden of melody.

The Keeper of the Precincts sat down in a great oak chair—all things in the place had the seals of age upon them—and drew Prince Starbeam towards him. The grasp of his hand sent a vibrant thrill through the soul rather than the body of the youth. He who, sheltered in a wood from wind and sun, has lain bare limbed upon cool brown earth may have experienced the same manner of contact, though not in the same degree. Prince Starbeam looked with worshipful eyes into the eyes which read the book of his own beauty. He who has stood upon the brink of a sheer precipice and has known the drawing power of a blue deep beneath may have experienced the same attraction, though not in the same degree. So draws the Soul of the World the world of the soul in man. But it was a fiery and loving soliloquy of eyes with eyes, in which it seemed at first to the youth that he was looking into the heart-abysses of the Beloved Kinsman, as into a sea without tide or motion. O the mystery of eyes in Faërie, for he was floating after through the sea of his own heart, or the blue orbs which gave him back word for word in the Haunted Well, he saying: "The voice which I heard in Faërie is thine and thou."

But the voice of the Keeper recalled him with such appeal as when star unto star utters speech through the spaces of magical night.

The Speech of the Soul in Faërie

"The Path of Kindness is the path to a crown in Faërie," said the Keeper of those Precincts. "I have known you, Prince Starbeam, from the old and the far time. You have loved and cared for my children, who have brought me news of your welfare. But a ring-dove came yestereve, whose life you once saved, telling of care and trouble, some change on the face of things and the weird of a falling House. I sent my messenger to bring you, for the heart is young in Faërie, and the heart can help."

He spoke as one who has descended the Golden Stairs, carrying glad tidings. But in the BOOK OF THE BLESSED LIFE, which is a book of many Hallows, and these are early and late, it is added at this point on the part of a faithful scribe: "I am sealed on the lips with knowledge, to have and to keep: I am sealed on the heart with wisdom, to get and to give: for the high ends of quest. Out of the CHRONICLES OF FAËRIE, out of the golden tongues and RECORDS OF THE COURT OF STARS, into remote echoes of earthly speech, the words are drawn. They were interpreted to the mind of Prince Starbeam by a law of permutation in music." The soul of the hearer opened; from beginning to end he told his tale of days, of the BOOK OF THE VOICES OF FAËRIE, the QUEST OF THE GOLDEN STAIRS, his father's failing quest, the Haunted Well and its Vision, the love delivered for love to the Beloved Kinsman. As one who knows that Faërie is a sacrament of good will, the Keeper of the Precincts listened. He rose when Prince Starbeam ended and passed to a corner of the room, where old books were scattered one upon another on a broad shelf. They were books of invocation, books of a golden magic, the true magic in Faërie, the voices of morning glories, the blessed bells of bindweeds, and the BOOK OF THE PROPHECIES OF FAËRIE. It was the last which the Keeper of the Precincts took down, a mammoth volume, written within and without and stamped with monograms of stars. He placed it under his arm, and taking Prince Starbeam by the hand, led him into a great hall of the mansion. He set the book upon a central altar or table of emerald, and opened it, shewing strange characters within, like the language of a Court of Stars. Maintaining the grip or token of hand in hand, he began reading in a clear resonant voice, pausing at regular intervals and listening to echoes about them which—like a chorus of many voices—made answer in

A Solitary Shrine in Faërie

oracles. Read me the verses of Faërie: to read is to see; but there is another manner of language which comes, like the soul, from afar: it opens the ears in music but does not open the mind till another river is crossed. So Prince Starbeam at that time understood nothing. At length the Keeper of the Precincts closed the book and returned with him whence they came, where he laid his hands upon the youth's shoulders and said to him, speaking in that ineffable oneness of eyes to eyes:

"The woe of the world is a stinging-nettle, and the secret is to clutch it. I have gone up the Golden Stairs, I have seen the Court of Stars, when the oracles sounded within. I am one who descends therefrom. It is yours to work out your calling in the faith of the Stars, to seek and perchance to find the Magic Ring."

The light died out of Prince Starbeam's eyes and life seemed ebbing from his heart as he thought of the Lady of Silence, the face of his world's desire in the Haunted Well. In the stillness there came to them a remote murmur, as of an open sea: it filled the hall with low music. He said only: "The woe of the world in Faërie is the woe of a wounded dove: I shall wound my dove in Faërie." He knew that the Lady of Silence had pledged him love for love in the light of shining eyes.

A Gospel according to Faërie

That Keeper of the Precincts made answer: "The sorrow of Faërie is like those morning mists which the sun dissolves. The stars watch you: the Court of Stars provides. The Book of Fate in Faërie is the book of the art of its ruling. Do you rule on your own part in the vow which binds you. The sign and the seal are on you by which your life itself has passed for a shaping of ends into the hands of another."

"To whom have I given so much? To my forest-brother. Ah, who is my brother in the forest?"

"Earth and sea cannot answer. Link up your chain, my

son. The Keepers of Records in Faërie will give you the next link."

It seemed for a moment the voice of the Beloved Kinsman, and Prince Starbeam said therefore: "I am server of servers in Faërie."

The Keeper of the Precincts left him for moments alone. Between such moments in Faërie a door may open into timeless spaces, and in the silence which followed Prince Starbeam passed unawares into a passionless gulf of being, alone with the love of his heart, apart from all the images. But the Keeper returned, bearing a large egg, intincted with living red, and a vase of herbs and strong spices. Now walking before him, he led the youth to a low arched door which opened on a steep descent by steps. They went down together, under the inviolate sky, and paused in a narrow path between wheat-fields flowing onward to the cliffs.

The Blood and the Life in Faërie

"This path," said the Guide, "goes straight to the cliff's end. There set the vase upon a rock, and the egg on the vase also: then fire the herbs and spices, using this flint and steel. So shall you enter Faërie. To the keeping of the Stars therefore and the coming of the King."

Prince Starbeam turned quickly, but the Keeper stepped back and was not, for the violet darkness received him. So the Prince went forward and came to the path's end, at the sheer edge of the cliff. I have come out upon a quiet shore and stood by an everlasting sea; but in the depth and the darkness far down the precipice it seemed to Prince Starbeam that he was aware of a sea of cloud. As one who looks towards Faërie with a heart of worship, he raised up the vase, saying: "To the Queen of the Kingdom in Faërie." But he thought of the Queen of his Heart.

A Midsummer Night's Mystery

VI

THE OPENING OF THE EYES IN FAËRIE

Faërie is seen in the heart before it is seen with eyes; but the heart and the eyes are love. "I have opened the doors of Faërie," says one of the faithful witnesses. "I have learned the knocks of entrance, the signs and the countersigns of those who go forth in peace. I carry my caper-spurge, and the rocks and the earth open. The sea has its spells; the sea has its greater mysteries: I have borne my sign-manual over the golden sea. But the words of power in Faërie are words of love." As a pilgrim of love, Prince Starbeam carried within and without all signs and sigils which shewed that he was prepared properly to be exalted into the World of Faërie. He set the vase upon a rock, as directed by the Keeper of the Precincts, and the star Jupiter shone upon the herbs and spices, which gave forth their spikenard fragrance. Among the herbs he embedded the mysterious egg; its shell glowed in the night-light; and the movement within it was like human blood coursing in a human frame. With flint and steel in fine he fired the herbs, and overpowered very soon by their influence he sank in a swoon upon the sward. Who shall say after what spaces of time, or amidst what music of darkness? But when he awoke at length there was a great Phœnix brooding with spread wings above his prostrate form, its white plumage like a ghostly crepuscule and its red eyes glowing close against his own pallid and fervent face.

Keepers of the Mystery in Faërie

Now Prince Starbeam had seen in his ravishment the face of a glorious spirit, like a Herald from the Court of

Stars, and betwixt the trance and the waking his mind confused the spirit and the bird together. He arose, as it seemed to him, in the wonder of this perplexity, and it was presently as though he were folded in living arms and passing through pure, cold air. But anon he was in the talons of the bird or resting between its mighty wings, high over a sea of cloud. He looked in front and behind, but all trace of that old, embattled house and of the shore itself had been taken back into the darkness. The stars glowed in the zenith, but began to dissolve in the East as a faint red tinctured the furthest verge. The clouds beneath him began to burn and glow; the morning mists were informed with light fire; and presently the sun came up, magnified and ablaze with dusky flame.

Before and After in Faërie

But still the spirit or the bird winged its way westward, though he saw nothing of his bearer. He seemed pillowed on a great white cloud, which scudded before the wind. There was land now below them: they had crossed that clouded sea or the pearl-white sea of cloud. Lakes and rivers, forests and heath-clad hills, vast meadows and silent wastes—all were passed over. Blessed are the openings beyond the hills, at sunset and sunrise, or when a harvest moon glistens between them. But when he who is to enter Faërie beholds the hills open, let him welcome the end of his travelling, however far away. The sun rose to the zenith; the sun watched therein and drew in fine to the West. The purple glory of dusk fell upon their tireless flight, and then far away, far over a wide water, far over woods beyond it there loomed a chain of hills. As the hills rose and parted, they passed between and beyond: the glades and glens, palaces and towers of Faërie unfolded to the West before them. The spirit or the bird dropped down, and the feet of Prince Starbeam touched the musical earth. Like the flight of a shaft had seemed that even course pursued through the day and the

Arrow and Mark in Faërie

night; and now the goal was reached. The end was like the beginning: a moment he seemed to be folded in the loving arms of a spirit; in a moment more he was alone, with a great moon above him.

There is a Palace at the centre of Faërie: it kept the distance before him, the moonbeams shining as if upon silver walls, on seven gates like gold and over the jewelled spires. Between the youth and the Palace were dim sweet groves, full of fragrance and melody. Like music also there came to him—from a far-off place within—the solemn words of his father and the high prophecies of stars. The way into Faërie is a word of sweetness, clothed in many forms of action: the path in Faërie is Kindness; goodness earns its gifts. Hereof are the high intimations which came to Prince Starbeam, as he passed on to the Palace. Bells of the cloisters of Faërie seemed to be ringing his welcome, while the life of that world without end gathered and scattered about him, amidst flashing of wings and sheen of jewelled robes. There were stately humanities of Faërie in royal and priestly vestments, in robes like gardens of flowers and spangled meadows of raiment. They hailed him and passed away. Palm-trees of maidens in Faërie, signed and sealed with beauty, carried their banners before him. There were spirits, moreover, who came from the world's end, from world's end in Faërie—the place where wonders finish and there is no story after. There were spirits from cities in waters, from palaces in lakes, cities of dream in Faërie and veiled cities in amaranth deeps of sea, or old houses bosomed in mountain pools. There were some that came from vast and silent halls of sunset, and some from coral gateways of the golden dawn, where peaches blossom at morning, far in the Holy East. From the four quarters of heaven they came and went, with stories to treasure in chronicles and boons to bear away. There were also those winged beings whose homes are in green fields, in streams and valleys, in still recesses of woods. There were those in fine who had travelled from crowded cities of men.

The roll of the years, the solemn roll of the ages, Prince Starbeam heard on the outskirts as far off rumours in measures, and he in a still duration—without dividing of times. He went up the path to the Palace. The Palace shone before the smouldered sunset, a thousand turrets and oriels grouped about seven great spires. He saw the vacant throne of Faërie, the sceptre of green malachite and suspended emerald crown. He saw the high hill behind the Palace; but it is known that the Golden Stairs may be there or here to-day and otherwhere to-morrow. He did not at that time behold the Golden Stairs.

The Palace of Art in Faërie

Had the birds and the bees sung his praises? Did the flowers tell them to the winds, which spread them over the whole world? But he was known and welcome on the hither side and the thither, wherever he paused or passed. Great is the state of fair maidens riding on quests to court: they fled before him in moonlight, making their hailing signs and music from ropes of hair, unbound beneath the stars. Wardens of gates stood and presented arms. There was reining of plunging steeds, as the gallant knights rode by, a giving of grips and tokens and watchwords of the time. He went up the steps of the palace and stood beneath the eaves. As if from a Court of Stars to acclaim a King in his coming, from a spire above the eaves one voice and its word of music fell on the heart of the Prince. Then and for ever henceforward he knew that out of old worlds of vision—whether on earth or in Faërie—unfolds the world beyond all seeing.

The Kingdom of Faërie

The song and the rapture ended; the bird took wing amidst the listening stars. Prince Starbeam entered the Palace and passed through a crowded court, where the light of the night was even as light of day, a glory of amber and gold. "Who keeps the archives of Faërie?" is asked by a Steward of the House in the waste and marish chase, he writing on one side of a faded cipher scroll. "I am only a clerk of the works, yet I have seen strange writings and the motion of great pens; but the scribes I did not see. Perchance the invisible days write their own story." He came to the book-rooms of Faërie and crossed thereafter certain inward chambers, where all the presences were unseen, so to a central place, on the threshold of which he knew that there were no presences, unless it might be one watcher, withdrawn on the further side. He passed over that threshold as he who lifts without breathing a curtain of woven light. That curtain fell behind him. He was aware of a place of the presence and of one in the light of her shining who was greater than a Keeper of the Precincts and brighter in her star-body than was he who came in the forest, the Beloved Kinsman. The Vision spoke in her splendour as the Spirit of a Star might speak and gave him welcome within, for the sweetness of manners in Faërie is like purple lavender. Who buys sweet lavender of Faërie, which is not bought for gold, but with love of a golden heart?

According to the Honour of Faërie

Prince Starbeam answered and said in his worshipful tones: "I am server of servers in Faërie. I am charged with a chain of doom and am sent to link up the chain, in the seeking—perchance in the finding—of a Magic Ring."

She was a Woman of the Stars in their glory of native light, and at her word he was seated towards her, telling his story of life as he told it in the Paradise of Birds. He thought in his heart, while he looked at the Star Lady, that of such are the faces which shine for some in a haunted well; but her eyes had a love in them which was greater than love of humanity, though he did not deem it greater than that which he saw in the eyes of the Haunted Well, when they gave their message in the silence and when the heart heard within.

Now, this was a Queen-Regent, appointed by the Court of Stars to rule in the Land of Faërie till the promised coming of the King. She rose at the end of his story and stood for a space with radiant hands enfolded and the majesty of indrawn eyes, as one who hears in a place that is very far away the counsel of a secret voice. Thereafter she said to Prince Starbeam, who had also risen, listening with glowing orbs: "The link in your chain is sent from the stars above to you on the quest below. You shall bear it hence on a further stage of your pilgrimage, which is to one who is older than I am, the Daughter of the Stars. It shall count as a seal of mission, a warrant of ends insured. I am she who conveys and gives on behalf of those whose vicegerent and spokeswoman I am. With this are you sealed on the forehead and shall carry the light thereof to her who is my sister and superior in a further place of the world. The next link in your chain is the Magic Ring."

I will provide, says Faërie

Kisses that rest on the lips are like wreaths of roses. But she kissed Prince Starbeam on the forehead and led him to a small door which opened on a windy and solitary heath. There was a narrow path before them, going over the heath upward, to a certain hill in the distance. This was the way he must follow, keeping northward, till he came to a lonely lodge—the abode of the Daughter of the Stars. Seal me with kisses of Faërie; kisses are talismans in Faërie: say and seal. The star of that Kiss on his forehead made glory about his face and shone on the path of quest. After such high manner the Queen Regent gave him God speed at parting. So standing transfigured, and dreaming rather than knowing the source of light, he said: "Honour and worship of life to the gift and the Giver for ever."

The Secret Paths of Faërie

She answered: "To the King, in the day of his coming."

"O Royal Lady," he asked, "where shall the King who is to come know truly concerning his Kinghood?"

"At the head of the Golden Stairs."

"Where shall the sacred mystery of love and the truth of a Haunted Well be revealed to the heart of longing?"

"Where two shall be found as one."

"And where shall one who is unworthy stand face to face again with the Beloved Kinsman?"

"In the light of the Magic Ring."

"I go to seek and to find the Magic Ring."

She gave him her radiant hands, and he bent over them, saying: "To you, O Lady, in worship."

She answered: "To you, my Prince, in Kinghood."

The door closed between them, and he was alone on the windy heath in the light of his shining. O Stars on the forehead in Faërie, with other wonders of vesture and high adornment, it is love that lights faces in Faërie, and they shine with their own light. This is my torch in the darkness and the world's end of woodlands. He followed the path of quest, pondering the last words of the Queen-Regent, dreaming of Kinghood in Faërie, questioning his own heart, in case it could tell him why he was as one coming at length into his own when he entered the Land of Faërie. The heart answered within him; and seeing that the hush of the darkness intimates deeper things than speech, many things answered without, in the pause of the wind's voice, and then in its organ-tones. In this manner, with little toil, he ascended the steep hill and looked eastward towards morning.

A door may shut behind one, a path may loom in front, an end may shine afar

VII

THE DAUGHTER OF THE STARS

Open, ye Gates of Faërie, and open wide, ye Portals, to let the dreamer through. The glory of this world passes away, but not the glory of Faërie. After the passing of many days, Prince Starbeam's journey ended, like a dream which deepens slowly towards a deeper dream. As the sun of that world went down he drew towards the middle point of a fragrant waste, where dwelt the Daughter of the Stars. The great plain encompassed him, and far off was the violet gloom of a forest on the verge of the Morning Land. The sense of open vastness was less than the sense of solitude, but it was a solitude of great consecration. O plover, flying plover—the silence was broken by the plover and bittern. No moon rose up that night, but stars seemed nearer, and the star on his forehead diffused its sacred light. The spirit within him was filled with a sense of awareness towards the sheltering providence of hidden life behind the still, manifested life about him. It was near midnight when he approached that lonely lodge where dwelt the Daughter of the Stars.

Of Homesteads in Faërie

There is always a refuge in Faërie, always a lodge therein, but this was a low cottage, built of a fragrant wood—like that of the cedar—and almost hidden in creepers. Prince Starbeam was crossing already a luxuriant plantation about it, when out of the timber porch there glided the figure of a woman, wearing a plain white raiment, girt about the waist with a blue scarf or cincture. Lift up your veils, ye Daughters of Faërie, children of melody, harp-strings of perfect being. Her raven hair was confined

Maids beyond Price in Faërie

by a tiara of gold and pearls: this was her sole ornament, save indeed the transfiguration of majesty. Fair of body and sweet of looks, give me the Women of Faërie. When this vision of beauty beyond our worlds of vision issued from the porch, she bore in her hands a large globe, of a substance like crystal but more radiant in its shining. She placed the sphere on a tripod which stood in the garden and near which there was a disc of burnished ebony. The hush of midnight held that holy world; the globe was bare to the sky, and Prince Starbeam saw that the stars above were reflected therein, while at the same time it seemed to condense their light, which issued from within as a brilliant silver beam and fell on the surface of the disc in the form of words—the Secret Language of the Stars. Like a light flame, the strange characters flickered on the black ground, and it seemed to Prince Starbeam that with the world itself it should be cheap to buy the wisdom which could read those words. The Daughter of the Stars watched them with intent and full understanding. Ever and rapidly the characters faded, being replaced by others, and the glow in their reader's eyes, as a glory of joy and intelligence, bore witness to the revealed messages and joy of light therein. At length she covered the globe with a veil and moved forward some few paces. A star on the forehead in Faërie: O dreams of its shining. The youth went forward to meet her, with the star on his temples, uplighting all the face.

"I am Prince Starbeam," he said, "and I come to you from the Queen Regent of Faërie."

"Wherein shall I help you, peerless Prince?" asked she who was Daughter of Stars. "The Regent Queen has gifted you beyond the dreams of glory, in the name of the Court of Stars."

"She has sent me to link up my chain, in the seeking —perchance, and the finding—of a Magic Ring."

"Ah, that is a gift which is worth both giving and asking; but first I must hear your story."

What else should the Stars have told you, O gracious Daughter of Stars, on this night of nights in his questing, whom Stars had spurred and led? She drew him to a seat on that low rustic bench, over against the tripod. But she still stood and again uncovered the globe, through which the light poured as before in ghostly words on the ebony disc.

The Written Tongue of Stars

During the first part of Prince Starbeam's story, the eyes of the Daughter of the Stars were fixed on these phantom scripts, continually forming and fading at her feet; but in the middle way of his romance she turned. The solemn loveliness of his face was revealed rather than heightened by the halo of light around it, from the lambent star above. The heart has its sigils in Faërie, and her cheeks whitened as she looked. A new light kindled in her eyes, but she did not look again at the youth. Afterwards her eyes dimmed, as now the story ended and at the same moment the characters faded utterly. She saw that the glass shone only with the faint essential light of a faërie crystal. She raised her eyes to heaven and found that clouds had covered the faces of the stars. Prince Starbeam also marked the sudden change and rising bent over the globe. The light from the star on his forehead fell thereon and glanced, a thin ray, on the ebony disc. The Daughter of the Stars uttered a low cry; she drew him from the glass, throwing the veil over it, and then led him into the cottage.

Books of the Prophecies of Faërie

"Your story," she said to him, "is one of strange election: it reminds me of certain things and others it tells me newly. I do not question that when the hour is with us I shall be empowered to give you the next link in your chain. But the time is not yet."

She led him to an inner chamber. It was a thatched

cottage in Faërie, and he who entered through its porch by the open door beheld a round mirror. It was a simple mirror to him who looked but once and an opening in a way that is known at the second time of glancing, while for him who went up that he might gaze stedfastly therein it was like a world beyond the worlds. But back of the world of vision is the world of the stillness, and the inner chamber was a place of still life, like a heart filled with the keen intentness of one most loving thought. In the centre was a table covered with spotless linen, and they sat down thereat. It is said in the BOOK OF FESTIVALS: "O fruit of the orchards of Faërie: I have dwelt therein and have feasted. I have drunk in the brew-house of Faërie and quenched my thirst from flagons of nut-brown mead. Faërie is a Cup of Nature pressed down and flowing over. It is drunk in strange taverns. I have called for meat and bread, and sacred food has been served me. The gates of death cannot prevail against it. I testify that those taverns are like a Secret Church of Faërie, and he who eats therein is he also who worships." At such a board and in such a high manner did the Daughter of the Stars refresh Prince Starbeam, himself in his shining a bright reflection and image of the High Court of Stars. But that which they ate was like fruit of the Tree of Life and food of odours, while that which they drank was wine of the grace of health, passing through lips in music.

Inns of Faërie

It is well in a manger of Faërie, or a stable under the stars, on a bed of down in Faërie or a palace of the King. O royal beds of vision and mysteries of sleep thereon: she shewed him an inner chamber, where there was a pallet of fresh flowers and sweet-scented herbs—plants of virtue, plants of power, seeds of the flower of gold and the perfect Herb of Sleep. Through all his dreaming and sleeping he was aware of the Daughter of Stars, but whether in spirit or flesh, that is, in the astral soul, which is the body of Faërie, is not in the BOOK OF THE RECORDS. It is told only that this deep and healing rest on a couch of flowers produced a secret change in Prince Starbeam's physical nature, so that he was fitted to have and to wear a Magic Ring. It was golden dawn at his waking: he knew of the change within and the new life of Faërie. Uprisen in light and fragrance, he saw a little door, somewhat low in the wall and standing open. Beyond it was a deep circular well, like a Bath of Psyche: he plunged therein and its many virtued waters completed the change within him.

The Pleasant Baths of Faërie

When he was clothed he passed into the outer room of the cottage, where was a great glory of sunlight, and greeted the Daughter of the Stars, who gave him welcome with the blessing of fathomless eyes. Great is the mystery of earthly womanhood, but greater and deeper still is the mystery of woman in Faërie. O faces full of spells: his own face shone in the morning light, but the star on his forehead was seen only in darkness, though the transfiguring effect remained.

Have you heard of sacred vigils in the hush of the Temples of Faërie? They ascended fasting to a Temple of the Stars, where the Daughter of Stars was Priestess. It rose on the summit of a hill, a reverence of mystic building. The Priestess took Prince Starbeam through Court and Holy Place into a Sanctuary within. He stood before the Altar, at a sacrifice of fire and song. With her also he recited kneeling the Secret Liturgy of the Temple, amidst smoke of ineffable incense. But the Altars of Faërie are not without their Chalices nor the Patens without their Bread. He ate of that Bread which is not made with hands and drank the Wine of the Sanctuary, burnt with hallowed fire from the shrines of the Seven Planets. So was he sealed within and without, in the heart and on the breast, with the Sigil of the Court of Stars. It was the day of his dedication, and when the

Ceremony was over they returned into the open air, to find an orange sunset fading in the West. "I have longed for thy ways in the morning and I have found thee in the Evening Star, thou world beyond the threshold." As they went down the hill, the light of that benign planet shone over them.

Feeding Dishes of Faërie

There was food of the earth of Faërie spread on the board of plenty; grail and cup waited. The star on his forehead began to kindle as the violet shadow of night brooded and deepened round them. "The Evening Star is Herald of the Court of Stars," said she who was their Daughter and Priestess. "It has brought us the Magic Ring. I called for it yesternight, singing in the Stars' Language, and I know that the gift is granted."

She took him by the hand and led him across the waste heath, where gorse of Faërie lifted its golden blooms. They came to a wych-hazel, which was withered on one side but young and green on the other. By the living side stood her tripod with the uncovered globe upon it and the ebony disc lying on the turf beneath. "Yes, it is here already," said the Daughter of the Stars. "The Magic Ring is with us and has worked the change which you see. Yet a little while, and this hazel will have found the life of youth."

The Coming of the Wonder

With reverent steps they approached the crystal globe. A beam of spiritual light passed through it, not falling on the ebony disc but into a single dewy blossom of the Agnus Castus. Prince Starbeam fell on his knees, while the Daughter of Stars, standing erect with wide-extended arms, invoked the Court of Stars. A single ray from the star on his own forehead mingled in the calyx with the stellar beam of the globe. The petals closed slowly; there was faint movement in the new leaves of the reviving tree; and the Daughter of the Stars bent and detached the bloom which enclosed the Magic Ring. Gently she removed the jewel from that now undying flower: every part of it rayed splendour and the whole circlet seemed cut from a single stone, far brighter than any diamond. So gems give light in Faërie. The Wise Lady placed it on Prince Starbeam's hand. Each into the eyes of each they looked, and the great worlds opened. Plead with me in the eyes of Faërie: she kissed him once upon the mouth on the part of the Court of Stars and once on her own part —perchance because she loved him who was himself in love with a dream. As they went back to the Temple on the hill, for thanksgiving to the Court of Stars and its radiant messenger in heaven, the youth said: "Will you teach me the Language of the Stars?"

"You may learn it on a day," was the answer, "but it will be without teaching. I am a Woman of Faërie, Prince Starbeam, and have learned it in the way of my race; but you must be first a King. So and so only can the speech of Stars be known by a man of earth."

"I will be a King then," he said in his quiet strength, as one who looks forward and sees.

"That is a good finding and true at the heart of things: but the time is not yet."

Muniment-Rooms of Faërie

There will be found in the CHRONICLES OF FAËRIE and in the RECORDS OF THE COURT OF STARS a full account of the night that Prince Starbeam, with the Daughter of the Stars, went up to the Temple of the Stars, giving thanks to them and to the Evening Star, fifteen days after he left the mansion of his father.

They deposited the immortalised blossom of the Agnus Castus in a secret shrine, where other storied flowers filled the place with odours. Their breath was like an offering of incense, their eyes as lamps in a sanctuary. Thereafter the Temple was left by another door, which opened on a further side of the hill, and from this point Prince Starbeam was to set out on his journey home.

"If I may," said Prince Starbeam, when they stood at the parting of ways, "I will ask you three questions."

"Ask and receive the answers, if nothing hinders the giving."

"When shall I see my Lady face to face?"

"On the threshold of Kinghood."

"Where shall I find the Golden Stairs?"

"I do not know: they move from place to place in the great work of quest."

"Who is the Beloved Kinsman to whom I was pledged in the forest?"

"I know but must not say. I cannot tell why he came to you: you may learn that before I do."

The Hand of God in Faërie

With earnest words of gratitude he exchanged the last farewell, and as he descended the hill with the light of his star about him, the Daughter of the Stars returned to the Temple; but neither looked back on the other, for the will of the Court of Stars stood as a wall between them, greater than any gulf which divides the life of earth from the Blessed Life of Faërie, or the body of this world from that of the astral soul. "O place of hidden humanities," it is said in an old script. "I tried all paths but love and never reached my end. I found the end at last in a path of love."

Lift me your veils, ye Daughters of Desire, Maids of High Degree: Children of Melody are harp-strings of perfect being

VIII

A WOODLAND CHAPEL IN FAËRIE

The Temple stood in the middle way of the wilderness, and thence it was a two days' journey to the borders. Beyond the broom and thyme, the date-palms of that region, there lay a cultivated country, meadows washed by streams and fruited gardens on the fringe of pools. The way back in Faërie is the way of a quest achieved, and through all that radiant atmosphere the Magic Ring put forth its plenary virtues within Prince Starbeam and about. Still lakes on the uplands reflected the sky above, and the stars wrote in the clear waters the old language of the stars. All tongues of earth are new in comparison therewith. Old legends transmitted from sire to son, through the ages and ages, were told by the passing winds. The whisper of a word from heaven moved among the bushes which bordered road and pool. Through saffron paths of the twilight, ways of violet, expanses of orange beyond, he came to that world's edge of cliff and the sea of white cloud below. There are gardens of this world and gardens also of dream, but beyond these—truest and best of all—is the garden of vision. On a mystery of height in Faërie, as it might be, in such a garden, he stood between the evening and the night-time. Over this pilgrim of love the moon of Faërie shone, and Faërie was in the heart of the lover. The peace of the quiet hour and the sheen of cloud beneath drew out his heart in rapture. A voice as of old ocean welled up from below the clouds, beyond all plummets and far beyond approach. That voice held him with subtle measures of intelligible speech.

The Purple Paths of Faërie

Wings of Rest and Healing

He was conscious no longer of virtue irradiating his body, diffused by the Magic Ring. He knew for a moment that there are other dreams than those of Faërie. All things outward passed and in a radiant state of mind, without effort or movement, he dreamed his path over the sea of cloud and thereafter returned to himself on the further side.

Henceforth at each step he was leaving the Land of Faërie further and further behind. The peculiar life of its atmosphere extends far beyond it through many a neighbouring realm; but now the pains of fatigue and the natural need of rest returned upon him. There is always a wood and it is ever a wood of mystery, which speaks the word of its mystery—a tongue by day and a tongue by night. There is always a place of repose, some cottage looking southward, a keep in the lonely waste, a homestead in the quiet copse. But seeking his rest and shelter, he entered on this occasion a darksome forest of fir-trees and came on a sudden in sight of a weather-worn chapel, hidden in a little hollow, overgrown with brambles. There also flourished the deadly nightshade, belladonna and monk's-hood, with other plants of bale, exhaling unhallowed incense in the dews and the darkness. Through narrow, lichen-crusted windows Prince Starbeam saw the place apparently deserted, and having forced his way through the undergrowth, the door yielded slowly to the pressure of his hand. But the facility of his entrance was due to the power of the Ring or the Star-gift of the Queen-Regent of Faërie, for the place was bound by a spell and the spell screamed as he opened, with the cry of a Queen of Spells, even the Queen Beryl, whose generations are declared in the BOOK OF THE STAR WORMWOOD. Faërie is White Magic, but there is also the Land of Sorcery.

A Mandrake's Cry

The air within was colder than the night of the forest. A small lamp hung by silver chains from the groined roof:

no oil burned therein, but a dusk gloom of light was diffused by a great beryl, enclosed in a crystal globe. Its rays fell upon an altar of black stone, inscribed strangely and supporting symbols belonging to unknown Rites. Turning from the altar and making no act of homage, Prince Starbeam saw in the middle North of the Chapel a catafalque of gridelin velvet, beneath which reposed the figure of a youth who was or seemed to be asleep. Prince Starbeam bent over him and the light from the star on his forehead fell on the young man's face, which was dark, impassioned and well-favoured. He touched the left arm, which was bare to the elbow, and found that he was contemplating a tinctured statue of marble. He looked in wonderment, as at a trophy of Art which put Nature to the blush, until a new thought flashed through his mind. The figure before him was stone indeed, but had not enchantment changed a human being into marble? This notion was confirmed by discovering that the youth's clothing was of ordinary fabric and his bow of supple wood. There are some who have seen with their own eyes the catafalques of Faërie and the veiled forms thereon: but they knew that the death was figurative. They have found also that there is no poison without some antidote and no spell without a counter-spell to dissolve it. The heart that is false maketh its own Faërie, and every spell therein is the utterance of a false word, expressed by mouth or in action. It is destroyed by its own antithesis, being a true utterance of speech or action in that sequence of events.

Of Hidden Statues in Faërie

There stood by the altar side a high-backed chair of old design, and this Prince Starbeam moved to the head of the seeming bier, where he sat down, deep in thought. The rays from the star on his forehead fell on that still face and there rested. After suspension of life in Faërie he felt that the sacred current must somehow flow again; and if the law of liberation is a law of act and will, he knew that the will was strong. That the purpose held in his heart was already in course of fulfilment, he did not learn or dream, till a wave of returning life, passing from head to heart, flushed the face of the statue, as the living warmth of the star-rays thawed that ice which bound the sleeper's senses. Once more the blood flowed, the heart beat, the breath came freely, and death was quickened for a time into living slumber. Prince Starbeam watched in wonder and gratitude the grace of this gradual change, divining how it was accomplished and bringing his own desire to work thereon. At length there was other movement: the eyes of the sleeper opened; raising himself on one elbow, he looked round; and his first words were: "Cynthia, Heart of Love."

Of Sleepers who Waken in Faërie

Prince Starbeam moved suddenly in great amaze; and the marble statue, fixing its startled eyes on his glorified face, cried between fear and wonder: "A Spirit of the Heights, a god: surely the spell is broken."

Prince Starbeam rose and standing at his full height could well have been taken for a spirit, or for that Beloved Kinsman to whom he had been pledged in the forest. He said notwithstanding: "I am human, even as you are." As he spoke, the star upon his forehead cast its light on the glowing beryl, which sent up a momentary gasping glare and so darkened. Wild ways of Faërie, and one of them is a way of the serpent: he knew now that the spirit of the place was evil, and taking his companion by the hand he led him through the low door into a moonlit glade, where they watched in silence a white vivid flame devouring that expended chapel. The youth looked again on the radiant face of his deliverer.

"You are surely some spirit descended from high heaven," he cried. "Your face shines with unearthly light: your star is of strange beauty. I would kneel to you, my saviour."

Prince Starbeam checked him, repeating: "I am of your human kindred; but I have lately come back out of Faërie."

"Thanks be to God for the omen," exclaimed the Sleeper Awakened. "What have you heard concerning the Magic Ring?"

"I was told of it truly as a gift of the Court of Stars."

"And what of the Princess Cynthia?"

"I bring no tidings back."

A time for question in Faërie: a time to ask and a time to answer: but blessed are the times of silence. The light of a dreadful suspicion dawned in the mind of the unknown. "Out of the Land of Faërie; out of that wonder-world; knowing the tale of my Lady: are you also her lover?"

Of a Space between Dreams in Faërie

He speaking passionately, a moment after remembered, as who should threaten his deliverer. He realised also that even if human like himself, the presence before him was wearing the glory of Heralds who come from the Court of Stars. "Forgive me," he said humbly. "If you knew the story of my love, you would indeed pardon."

That old story flashed through Prince Starbeam's memory. It told how the Royal Maiden of the Golden Isles had loved a Prince in the past time, but the Lord Royal had dismissed him for the want of a Magic Ring; and then that Prince went forth to seek it but was never heard of after. Was it possible that the youth before him was an actor-in-chief of this story? And what of his own past? Was it his to link up a chain for the sorrow of two lovers? He was pondering deeply in the heart upon this trouble when the eyes of the Sleeper Awakened fell on the Magic Ring. His face whitened and he uttered a despairing cry. "You have it, great Heaven of Stars," he moaned. "Will you steal the Star of my Life?"

The Love of Woman in Faërie

The voice of a dole to come was moaning also in Prince Starbeam's heart. His pace quickened as they went, at random through a wailing wold. His companion pointed to the Ring, saying: "Am I wrong? Tell me"—in imploring tones.

"How should I tell?" Prince Starbeam answered in asking, as one who is choked by words.

At that moment the Star faded from his forehead and its light from his face. Though not beyond all borders and past all hallowed precincts, they had reached at last the untinctured air of earth, where lights of Faërie dwindle, and lights from the Court of Stars return to heaven which gave them. The change terrified his questioner, who shrank back in the darkness beyond the moonlit way—as though he in his passionate woe had put out a light of heaven. Prince Starbeam felt for the first time that the night was cold, he stricken and far from home. He heard the distant wolf howling in the forest. There is love in the heart of a wolf for those who have earned it, but love had gone back through the vista. He stood with clasped hands. A snake glided from them through the undergrowth, and now as they drew together the moon silvered sadly the green water of a still pool beside them.

"All things are wrong between us," said the Sleeper Awakened. "Would that we had never met: my contact darkens your beauty. Would that I had remained a statue. Begone, lest I force from you that shining gem: its lustre blots out my life."

"Stay," said his companion, "and rave not thus. It is near morning and the weariness of a world is upon me. Let us rest somewhere. I must hear your story, that I may learn your claim on this Ring."

The warm blood flushed in the other's face, as he fell back, moaning: "What claim have I? Except that I love the Princess, and I pray that she loves me still, though I know not if moons or years have slipped through in my enchantment."

"What claim also have I, who do not love the Princess?"

"Do not love her? The Rose of the World in Faërie. To see is to love." *O Rosa Florescens*

"I have never seen her," Prince Starbeam said in his detachment.

The eyes of the Sleeper Awakened fixed him in doubt and wonder: "Why then did you go in search of the Magic Ring?"

"To link up a chain which the Stars put into my hands."

"And is it the will of the Stars that you should wed the Princess?"

"The stars in heaven forbid." But he, looking upward, saw how a star fell.

"It is you who have a story of stories," the Sleeper Awakened pleaded.

"Perchance it depends on your own, and perchance the time is not yet."

O vigils on the threshold and sleep within the precincts. They came to a fallen tree. An amber light tinctured the leaves above them. Far over villages and fields the dawn had broken: it began to penetrate the forest. The eye of the morning in Faërie looked upon them. They sat down together, with the night-dew heavy on their garments—they looking towards the lightsome day. And the Sleeper Awakened told his story of doom.

Wayside Chapels of Roses: the aisles and the arches, the red pillars and the white

IX

THE HISTORY OF PRINCE MELNOR AND OF BERYL, A QUEEN OF SPELLS

I am a son of the King of the Isle of Palms; my name is Melnor; and strange things were prophesied concerning me, not only by wandering sibyls and those who read in the stars but by all and sundry who found that such devices led to the royal favour. Now, there came on a day to the palace a certain worshipful stranger who spoke darkly concerning talismans of flowers, of secrets hidden in flowers and flowers that speak in the heart. He said also that I might live to be a true man and even a great King; but I must be preserved from the false troth in Faërie and the doom of its keeping at the hands of a Queen of Roses, who was also a Queen of Spells. The age of eighteen would be that of liberation from danger, so only that I was watched till then. The warning was accompanied by a very plain censure of my present mode of training, after which the stranger departed with empty hands, seeking nothing from royal bounty. There was much anxiety concerning him and his words of power. My parents conceived many plans to amend their ways, which were errors of kindness only, and for my better preservation I was put to be trained in a tower of cedar and ivory, apart from the rest of the palace. Of the prophecy itself I was kept unhappily in ignorance, lest curiosity on my own part should somehow prove my ruin. Moreover, no rose was permitted to bloom, even in the vicinity of the palace. These were great precautions surely. O mystery of treasures and guarding of treasures in Faërie; but there

Women of Bale in Faërie

Watch-Towers of Temptation

is a window open somewhere or a door is left ajar. All went well notwithstanding until I was seventeen, at which age I was a fair-grown youth, fond of all active exercises and utterly nauseated with my strange, secluded life, its circle of enforced study, the dull masters of sentences who shadowed all its ways and the narrowness of its few pleasures.

I had a passion for hunting and found some rare opportunities to gratify this taste under my father's careful eye. He taught me to pursue only the nobler game, especially those beasts of prey with which neighbouring forests abounded. On a time, however, and it was very soon after my birthday, we returned unsuccessful from a long boar-hunt. I was vexed out of measure and certain pages in our train felt the effect of my humour. We were about two miles from the palace when a brace of young doves, startled from their covert by the passing cavalcade, flew over our heads towards open country on the left. I raised my bow in sheer wantonness and shot them one after another. They were picked up riven by the great shafts, and my father, who witnessed the exploit, was so incensed at this cruelty that he rebuked me in public—to the gratification no doubt of my pages. Next day I was alone in the high-walled garden of the tower, having passed the morning in tormenting the pages for their brief triumph. I flung myself on a rustic seat, when a large bird with plumes incarnadined perched before me on an apple-tree and began dressing its splendid feathers. A stranger in the garden and country, it was far handsomer than all I had seen on wing. I stretched out my hand, hoping that it would alight thereon, but it changed quickly from bough to bough, pursuing the same task. At last, weary of coaxing, and out of temper again, I was glancing about me for some sharp missile to cast, when the bird came—with a little graceful circling flight—and perched of its own

The Flight of a Red-Winged Bird

accord on my shoulder. Very gently I smoothed those glossy plumes, the bird bending its beautiful head and glancing with large, speaking eyes into my face. My heart beating with apprehension lest the creature should fly suddenly away, I went slowly towards the tower. There was no attempt to escape, only a smooth beak laid gently against my cheek—as if kissing me. I entered the ivory tower through a small door at the back, where—to my shame and almost terror—an unknown tormentor had hung the mangled doves from a peg in the wall. It was something like a voice of doom which said quietly in my ear, but on the other side of the red-winged bird: "The soul flies, and the dove is a soul in Faërie." And again: "The dove is also a messenger, bringing tidings and high tidings, all the way from Faërie,—so far and so near." Passing hastily, with averted, reddening face, and ignoring exclamations of astonishment which the living bird excited, I hurried through the open door and reaching my own apartments, drove out the pages roughly, to enjoy my treasure undisturbed. My fondest caresses were lavished on the beautiful, red-feathered creature, who received and returned them, as with human affection and intelligence. The news spread through the palace and reached the ears of my parents, who visited me in my seclusion, to behold the prize. They were astonished at its beauty and raised no difficulty, though I have wondered since whether scales fell later from their eyes. A gold stand was provided from the royal aviary, and this I placed in my bedroom, where the bird roosted at night. I became from day to day more enamoured of this new favourite, though it was neither useful in the chase, nor gifted with the power of song.

The Opening of Doors in Faërie

During these hours and their sorcery, my pleasure was overcast always by the presence of the withering doves, which still hung by the door, and whenever I passed unwittingly that secret voice sounded with an ever varied message: "The wisdom of doves in Faërie," and yet again: "The voice of the dove is the voice of a spirit in Faërie." But the pride and the shame held me, so that I did not order their removal or the discovery and punishment of the offender. At last in the dusk of the sixth day, I tore them madly from the wall and heaved them forth among the rubbish. They passed away, as it seemed to me, with a wailing cry, and then for the last time that voice pealed in my ears: "The Blessed Spirits have warned from the gate of woe. The gates of sin open. When shall the gates shut?" I thought that the walls were archives and that windows spoke in chronicles.

The Vigil of Birds in Faërie

On the evening of the seventh day I noticed a curious alertness in my favourite, and this continued till my attendants departed finally, after which she grew perfectly quiet but all the while seemed watching me with more than usual intentness. I sat down to unstring my choicest bow; a large lamp was burning on a table before me; my back was turned to the bird, for I was somewhat absorbed in the task, when I heard a movement behind me, followed by a slight musical laugh. Looking round, I saw to my bewilderment, in the half-light at the furthest corner of the room, the figure of a woman in red, a maid of high degree, whose bright eyes were turned towards me with an arch expression. O mysteries of womanhood in Faërie. I saw also that the bird was missing and divined that some magical transformation had occurred. I must have stared awkwardly at this unexpected apparition as she advanced into the full light, where she enchanted me as much with her beauty as I had been drawn previously by the bird's brilliant plumage. I know not what words passed, for I had spoken to few women and for a moment was almost frightened. She reassured me in winning tones and gave me presently a beautiful crimson flower, the enfolded petals of which—circle within circle—were a thousand times more fragrant than the lilies of my own garden. I dream of it now and ever, that flower which is laid on the heart and of things that it tells in secret. She counselled me to conceal it in my bosom, since the world of love is also a world of silence.

Counsels of Remembrance in Faërie

There are gems that travel in Faërie and gems that speak: I learned that she was Beryl, a Queen of Spells and of Roses, whose dominion was in a far country. Of the race and royalty of Faërie, she had native powers beyond the gifts of man and had been trained otherwise in the art and craft of magic. She had seen me in her glass of vision and learning that I was isolated in a tower of cedar and ivory, apart from all joy of roses, she had assumed the form of a bird at her own risk and peril, to bring me the choicest flower of which she was queen and mistress.

My initiation into the mysteries of the rose filled me with love for my instructress, but I learned with dismay that because of the law of enchantment she could come to me in her true shape once only in seven days, when, however, she would always present me with a fresh rose —more fragrant, if possible, than the last. The night melted in rapture, but towards morning the magnetic eyes of Beryl cast me into soundless sleep. When I awoke, the bird was on her stand and came to me for my morning caresses.

Henceforth I was a changed being; the visible world presented itself under a new aspect, in this grace of a woman of Faërie and her topaz-light of tresses. Its vistas were filled with the halo drawn from the damask petals of the secret flower. The hidden language of its odours, the spells of its incense-breathing filled me with unutterable longing and fed me from a tree of knowledge. But about this time there was an unaccountable withering of white lilies surrounding the ivory tower.

Food of Witchcraft in Faërie

As in a place of the hiding of roses and under their

covenants of secrecy, the visits of Beryl, Queen of Spells and Roses, continued for a whole year, and then I was told that she must leave me, but it should be only for a brief space. The strength of my passion implored her, but there was her own safety and there was also our future happiness—a concurrent compulsion. The strength of my love urged her, and I learned then that the Law of Enchantment, which is blind, required her to resume her natural shape, to ignore which would be to remain always a bird. This silenced my entreaties and the next day the bird was missing. As I made neither search nor clamour, it was concluded that I had wearied of my favourite, and as such is the way of life in courts there was no one to care or wonder. At eighteen my birthday was celebrated amidst great rejoicing, since it was thought that Fate had been overruled in my favour. I was released from my long captivity; the story of the strange prophecy was at last told by my parents, who rejoiced with themselves and me on the fortune which had crowned their efforts. I kept my own counsel in a heavy heart, amidst dark foreboding that the promised misfortune stood already on the threshold—an hour that would come in Faërie, a dread and fateful day.

The Flight of Women in Faërie

As days changed into weeks, the weeks into months, with no news from my lady, her absence and the indwelling prophecy brought me into a state of dejection. A woman coming out of the unknown and a woman returning thither, her image remained with me as of a beautiful, insidious enchantress who had doubtless changed or forgotten, and though the delight of her magical roses was ever fresh in my remembrance, I began to look on her as one who might yet be my ruin. Buffeted in that direction, I was torn also in another, with fruitless desire for her return, remembering the old ecstasies and hoping in the heart's sophistry that her presence might find me a way of escape from that which her coming threatened.

It is only for evil in Faërie that walls a prison make, whether of stone or steel; and I was now in a prison of the spirit, built about me in my own mind, when a way of escape opened; but it was truly the way of doom, a way of pictures and portraits, unknown faces, like other worlds in a mirror. Among those who sought in vain for a Magic Ring in their love for the Princess Cynthia, there was an artist who lost his reason. He went about the world—as he may still indeed be going—and bore his lady's portrait, so that all men might love her and then prove therein no less wretched than himself. On such a mission he came to the Isle of Palms and singled me out in secret as one of his victims. To the eye and its light in Faërie, at the shrine of those radiant eyes, with a new hope in my heart, I knelt in worship. The tarnished image of the Queen of Spells and Roses fell to pieces, and its shards crumbled into powder. Not only the magic of beauty but all the magic of quest opened its world about me. I would find the Magic Ring and wedded to Princess Cynthia that dark old prophecy should carry its baleful message over the verge of things. My troubled and haunted moods had not escaped my parents, and there had been much care in consequence. Whatever they thought of the Magic Ring or its seeking, there was nothing more desirable than to enter into closer bonds with the Lord Royal of the Golden Isles, and could their son be married to his daughter this end were gained. The alliance must be welcome on his own part, and if the Magic Ring was not indeed a fable, the vain research of its counterpart had taught perhaps their lesson. It came about therefore that with many gifts and a great retinue, I started for those islands.

The Quest of a Bride in Faërie

At the long journey's end I have reason to think that the Lord Royal received me more graciously than had befallen others, though I learned speedily that the rumoured condition tolerated no alternative, whatsoever the suitor's claims. Yet I was permitted to linger at court, seeing and communing with the Princess Cynthia. My love and devotion grew from more to more, and she came to love me in return. This was no sooner discovered by the Lord Royal than I was commanded to leave his dominions, nor ever return except with the Ring of Marriage. So was the Princess forbidden the only suitor for whom she had learned to care; so in her youth and her beauty was she brought to question the Ring, to challenge the joy of the gift; and for me in exchanging the last tokens of fidelity, it seemed that my doom was upon me.

The Ring and the Troth in Faërie

When it tore me at length from her presence, I mounted my horse and sending back my retinue, set forth on my quest alone, resolved to win and to wear a Magic Ring or never revisit the land of my home and inheritance. Whither should turn the quest? Who should declare its path? I rode on a chance forward, apart from light or plan. All ways were forward. It came about at the grey close of an evening late in spring that I reached a little hermitage. The peace of its precincts felt like a quiet night and an only hope of rest. I was welcomed by an ancient man, whose kindly manner and sweet repose in dignity drew me to open my heart and pour out its griefs before him. But who shall express my wonder when he discovered himself as that worshipful stranger who had once prophesied concerning me? Surely he knew beforehand all that I told in folly; but he sorrowed with me in his wisdom at my parents' futile precautions and so proceeded to counsel. He prayed me to watch and to work for the flight of the evil days, that cannot endure in Faërie. A gate of doom had been opened by other hands than mine, and although I had been drawn within, for him who stood at the threshold a retreat was still possible. There was one way to avoid the dole which threatened me: it was to

And Mercy the Key of the Treasure-House

Of Heirship in Faërie

renounce my present quest, going back to my father's Kingdom, where I might look shortly to inherit crown and throne. A gate should open there and a path should lead therefrom, with a high prize at the end of a joyous journey. But I told him of my heart's devotion and yet more fully of her who loved me in return. "Why do you praise that course which means the grief of both?" I asked.

He answered: "For two reasons. In the first place, however hard your separation may seem now, it can bear no comparison with that woe which would follow your union; and, in the second place, you who have received and cherished the gifts of a Queen of Roses can never by your own effort obtain the Magic Ring."

This verdict annihilated all my hopes. Impotently I accused Beryl as the cause of all my misfortunes and cursed the witch who had betrayed me. When this phrensy broke in tears, the Hermit said solemnly: "In a BOOK OF THE WISDOM OF FAËRIE, a book of the deeds of old, it is written thus: 'I broke my sword on the Gates of Faërie; they came and drove me away. I laid my heart on the steps of Faërie; they opened and took me in.' I bid you return to your parents, in the name of love and duty. A great danger threatens them."

But I cried in my rage bitterly: "I have no parents now. They too have been a cause of my ruin, by keeping me in darkness on my danger. From this moment I disown them."

Love is the Marrow of Faërie

"The dread at the heart of Faërie is dread of the base heart," the Hermit said in his gentleness; and I flinched before him, nor yet at the words only but because of a change which came over him, so that he looked now in his majesty like one of the Wise Masters or a Messenger from the Court of Stars. As those who have power, at once in word and deed, he spoke also with majesty and yet as one who would persuade, saying: "I will plead with you in the name of my mission and of the Twelve Houses of Heaven. There is one who is called and chosen for the Throne and Kinghood of Faërie: not yours to reign therein; yet can you win your place. I proclaim the Mystery of the Bells and the sea of cloud. A day shall come, nor is it perchance remote, when folk shall go out and come in, passing from hither to thither over the sea of cloud, and Kings of the Precincts shall administer the Golden Rule of Faërie, on this side of the world. Lay the message to your heart: abide thereby, and I who am their faithful witness will pledge the stars to watch over you."

But the wrath had hardened my soul, and I said only: "Vengeance on the base enchantress who has poisoned my life. Thereafter I may consider what you tell me."

It came about that I rushed from the cottage and, having found my horse, mounted. The Hermit stood at the door, as when he welcomed me in.

"What danger threatens my parents?" I turned and asked. But he answered: "The stars have spoken. The voice of the Stars has called. That which remains is yours and devolves on you."

His hands were raised towards me—whether to drive me forth or perchance in prayer, I know not to this day. I said then in my anguish: "Is there no hope of my finding the Magic Ring?"

He answered, pronouncing sentence: "By your own efforts, none," and shut the door upon me.

Sorrows of Prodigals in Faërie

It was the first hour of the morning, and I rode sadly away, allowing my horse to choose his own path. I was as one who goes forgotten in the numbering of Faërie. Having no notion of that which menaced my parents, I sought to persuade myself that they would find means to evade it. Moreover, I was a living example of the fools who strive with doom: should that overtake them, I could be witness but not saviour. Perchance I cheated myself and perchance knew it; but in all events and any I resolved to seek Beryl, not that I knew of her Kingdom, its name or place, and not that in highways or byways a thousand askings opened a door to knowledge. I came at length to this wood and discovered that lonely temple, the scene of my late enchantment. I found also the couch of skins and, seeing the place deserted, decided to call it a refuge for the time being and live as I could by hunting. There was rest when the night came and it was sweet to the bones that ached from the hard and humid beds in woods and forests. But about midnight an uproar in the temple awoke me, and I saw Beryl standing over me in royal robes, looking more beautiful than ever, though her face was inflamed with rage. It filled me with a certain fear, a certain homage for the magnificence of her baleful aspect, an unwitting sense of worship. Had she passed there and then from the high estate of wrath into that of the old kinship, it may well have been that, at least in the time of her presence, amidst her atmosphere of spells and roses, I should have forgotten the Magic Ring, because of her living sorcery. But she railed at my faithless ways and heaped on me her bitter scorn, because I could withstand no hour of trial. And then I flamed also, though it seems to me that the words were weak, crying that she had abandoned me and that I had waited a whole year.

Places of Anathema

"A year," she echoed bitterly. "Was that so long to debar you, for whom I worked more than for myself in the time of absence? But do not hope to deceive me: I know your recent pursuits; I know your passion for Cynthia: but there at least I baffle you."

In pure dread of my undoing and with a foretaste of coming doom, I screamed at her all my charges, the sorcery which she had worked upon me, the prophecy which she had planned to fulfil, my everlasting loss through her in the Quest of the Magic Ring, her fatal and terrible roses, and the perfection of my new love, to which I looked for salvation.

A Lip of Truth in Faërie

The roses whitened on her cheeks, as a yet more deadly fashion of light blazed suddenly in the eyes, which fixed upon me. She uttered no word of answer, but presently with outstretched hands, turning to the altar, she hissed rather than spoke, in a strange and secret tongue. It came to me that there was death in her hands when afterwards they were held above me, the anathema of her whole being streaming from shapely fingers. A deadly chill benumbed my limbs and crept over my whole body. I strove to rise in vain—to speak, but my tongue was stone. As in a few moments, the fell change was effected and the sentence of her witchcraft rang in music through my ears: "Thus shalt thou remain, a statue, till she who is Queen in Faërie by a Kiss dissolves the spell."

There are those who sleep in enchantment and those who wake therein. Was this the promised misfortune? But you will see at least that the dread of it was beyond all common modes, for through long daylight hours the mind was at work within me, though I could not speak or move. Sleep is the light of the soul in the World of Faërie, and sleep or some trance-state came in the dark to save. You also came as my saviour in the vision of sleep at night. Do I wake indeed or dream? And how was the spell dissolved, if perchance I am free from its toils? That it was not by the Kiss of a Queen in Faërie may, I think, be the sign that Beryl has lost her power.

A Death in Life of Faërie

"You are mistaken," said Prince Starbeam, as the Sleeper Awakened ended. "The Queen-Regent of Faërie kissed me on the forehead at parting as a link in my chain of quest. Like a star it remained with me; as a star it lighted my way: when the light of it shone upon you, the evil spell dissolved."

"You are my deliverer indeed," Prince Melnor said; "but the anguish endures within me. Yours is the Magic Ring, and I am very sure that the Lord Royal of the Golden Isles will give you his elect daughter. But what of that gift when the heart is otherwhere? She is mine and mine and mine: I swear that her heart is with me, even in the night of spells. . . . And now you have heard my story: what of your own, I pray you?"

"The time is not yet," said Prince Starbeam. "Let me think for a while on yours, for a space of sleep in my weariness. There is a veil on the secrets of Faërie, but he who lifts shall see; and the time for the lifting of veils is the time of sleep for me."

"Take my cloak," said Prince Melnor. "I am in no mood to rest, and so will watch beside you."

Prince Starbeam took the cloak and wrapping the folds about him, lay down upon the grass. The watcher sat near him, with eyes fixed upon his face, from which all the glory had faded but the native light of being, the beauty of spirit within. He knew not the time of this watching or at what point his heart went out to the sleeper; but Prince Melnor's eyes were fixed suddenly by a slant sunbeam falling on the Magic Ring. A moment would remove it and immortal youth, beauty, happiness in the possession of Cynthia would follow on that act. He sprang to his feet and hurried a little distance apart. There he threw himself on the ground, buried his face in green, fragrant herbs, and shut out all sounds with his hands, for all that is evil about the precincts of Faërie was goading him on to infamy.

Of Pledges taken on Mystic Herbs

Meanwhile Prince Starbeam was pondering on things heard and seen with the mind's eye in the tale of the Sleeper Awakened. He saw very clearly from what central point of self came all its springs of action; that in the human order of things—apart from spells and roses—

Prince Melnor and Beryl might well be meant for one another; and in 'fine that the Court of Stars had intervened to forbid his union with Princess Cynthia. What, on the other hand, meant in the chain of things her prolonged love for Melnor? What of his own part, which bore no part in her? Was he to come between them on the claim of a Magic Ring and cast out his own love? The vista was hidden with clouds at a hand's breadth before him; but one thing loomed plainly—that not by an act of his must the Sleeper Awakened receive that Gift of Stars. In such thought he fell asleep. The Key-word of Faërie is Love, and Beloved is the word in flesh. He was walking presently through a vista, with a great light about him and the arms of the Beloved Kinsman.

The Sacred Key of Faërie

The Vision said to him: "Another link of the destiny. Link up your chain, my brother: but the way is long to the Kinghood. In the light of the Magic Ring I have come, and my charge is with me."

Prince Starbeam said: "I have watched long for your coming, as in age-long vigils of Faërie."

"I am ever at the street-corner, in the next room of the house, on the other side of the veil which clouds the eyes."

"Without doubt we have walked together, but I have not seen you; and at the great distance we could not be further away."

"Can the sight of eyes make nearer? I am you in your sorrow and you also in joy, to still and to stay."

"Take away scales, I pray you: lift up the veils which cloud; and let us go forth together, wherever your charge may lead."

"The charge shall lead to the goal, but I shall walk unseen till the day of the harvest of eyes. The charge shall not fail of its goal, whatever the thorns between."

"Give me your charge therefore."

"And give on your part, my brother, the Magic Ring to Prince Melnor, for that is the next link."

"This shall be done, my Kinsman, though I see no longer the path but its thorns only."

O deeds of gift in Faërie and the years in which they mature. The Vision bent over him, so that they were face to face in the blankness of all things else. The eyes of the Beloved Kinsman and the light beyond light of those eyes welled over into the eyes of the dreamer. And it was thus—as it might be—for a moment or a timeless gulf of rapture.

Gifts and their Price in Faërie

When Prince Starbeam woke and rose up, he found that Melnor had left him and was asleep at a little distance. He placed the Ring upon his hand, and the hand closed over it, but at this moment the Sleeper did not awaken. Prince Starbeam looked round him, deep in thought. He said, with a faint smile: "I link up my chain strangely: I had better go back to my father."

He set out accordingly, looking to find his way. But of his story up to this point, let it be marked well that it had not been told to Prince Melnor.

O far-off things, and eye of the mind in Faërie

X

A DAY OF PASSING IN FAËRIE

In the CHRONICLES OF FAËRIE, in the BOOK OF THE BLESSED LIFE, and in the RECORDS OF THE COURT OF STARS, there are some who have seen with their own eyes the date of Prince Starbeam's return to the House of his father in the waste and marish chase, fifteen days after he parted from the Daughter of the Stars, making the time of his absence in all thirty days, as a moon of hidden life. He had heard strange birds in the wilderness, singing of eternal things; wind-words about the harvests of Faërie; the pipes which are answered all over the forest and fell. He had seen the flight of darkness in Faërie and the blithe elevation of heart in all that loves the light. The bank of wild thyme is ever a place of vision: he had slept and dreamed thereon. Keeps among remotest mountains; inaccessible peaks and temples that loom above; towers that hold their age-long vigil over unfathomed depths of precipice: he had tarried and communed with them from afar on his homeward way.

The stars had watched him in his passing, and the stars began to kindle over the sea, as yet once more he stood at the door of the House, in the old porch. That garden salved from the waste by his early care and love was slipping again into the waste, and whether or not the birds had fled their bowers, he heard no evensong. So also, notwithstanding a remembered covenant, the lamp was not burning in its high turret to warn all ships at sea. The door of the House stood open and the halls were dark within. The air was damp and heavy; the silent imme-

I have sung at Strange Vespers

morial ghosts withdrew from corridors and stairways, as he passed from room to room and so to that of his father, where an aged Usher of the House whispered him in and retired. As he enters hushed in heart, the shadows are lost and found, the shadows move and change in the sorrowful light of tapers about the Master's bed. The hand of death was upon him; the shadow of death was between the vapours of darkness; and the eyes of the ghostly watcher were amidst the flickering lights. As the flame of the tapers rose and fell incessantly, so ebbed and flowed a remnant of mortal life in the wasted frame. Did he think of that Bright Land under a Bright Sky, where once his sires had dwelt, according to the Legends of the House? The House which cannot be reached is the House which comes in Faërie. The Town walks over the Wold. Perchance the Bright Land was nearer now than ever in failing quests, followed on earth and sea; perchance he began to discern that it is sought after another manner. Soft were the feet of his son, moving over the intermediate space; but ears of death are quickened, and the soul at the point of its passing heard and turned and saw. On the pillows of the couch the soul raised up its body, and hollowly the soul's voice seemed speaking within the frame, as the Master said in his agony: "Because I cannot reach you, hasten. I am lame and stricken: come to me therefore quickly."

Prince Starbeam came and knelt, with hands clasped on the tarnished gold of drapery and head over hands bowed.

"Have you wrought for the House and its glory? Have you fought for the end and crown? Have you brought the Magic Ring?"

The Yoke of Life in Faërie

"I have been on the Quest of the Ring and to link up a chain of life, O Father of mine. I have seen a Keeper of the Precincts, commissioned from the Court of Stars.

I have entered the World of Faërie and seen the vacant throne and the crown of its King to come. The Queen-Regent of Faërie sealed me with light on the forehead. I have seen the Daughter of the Stars. The Magic Ring came down from the Evening Star, and she who is Daughter and Priestess of the Twelve Houses of Heaven prophesied concerning my Lady and that standing on the threshold of Kinghood I should see her face to face. But the last link in my chain was a charge in vision to surrender the Magic Ring: it has therefore passed to another, and I come with empty hands, but looking for the glory of the House in another and greater Kingship than that of the Golden Isles."

As the Master of the House fell back, the arms of his son held him. The face of the dying man shone with light suddenly, and his voice rang through the chamber: "The World of Faërie is the Bright Land lying under a Bright Sky, where once our race abode. Are you called to the Kinghood of Faërie? Speak and say, my son."

"I have heard the call of the Quest; I have followed the calling voice. It sounds in the four quarters; it sounds and draws them in who are meant for the freedom of Faërie. On what other threshold of Kinghood shall I find my Lady of Dream? For the Princess Cynthia, she who is world's desire without the walls of Faërie, belongs of law to another; and not unto me, my father, is the royalty of the Golden Isles."

A Dream of Kinghood in Faërie

"O City of Morning Light on the hither side of the hill. Part me the curtains of darkness and let me see thy world: through gates of gold in Faërie, gates of the sheen of gold."

A silence fell in the room; the air grew cold suddenly—all tapers burning low. Prince Starbeam said at last: "Father of mine, faithful and true father, I crave a blessing on the work."

The eyes of the dying man had closed, and now the eyes opened. His pale, thin hands sought the head of his boy, and there rested. Lifting up his eyes to heaven he called down on Prince Starbeam the gifts of blessing and of Kinghood from the Twelve Houses of Heaven. The words which he used stand shining in the RECORDS OF THE COURT OF STARS, but few can render the symbols; they have been seen in the CHRONICLES OF FAËRIE, but they are written in an unknown tongue. Yet a witness is borne in the BOOK OF THE BLESSED LIFE and in the BOOK OF THE VOICES OF FAËRIE—have you turned the leaves thereof, between its cedar covers?—that amidst the words of the blessing a great star, as it might be, the span of a man, kindled in the dark room, with five keen points of light, growing from more to more, while the voice and benediction lasted. And having blessed his son, the Master of the House died. Then it was dark of dark, and the fatherless Son of the House swooned on his knees, with the still hands benumbed on his head. The Usher of the House found them. His care restored the orphaned youth and led him from the death-chamber. In his own room the mighty pageants of the immediate past opened the gates of memory convened about the Passing of the Master, and the tears which followed after left a heart free.

The Mystery of Death in Faërie

They prepared the body of the Master for his cold bridal of the grave. "Lay me not down at the West: I would look to the East in Faërie." Was it Death on a white horse which rode through the marish chase in the light of the setting moon? Was it Death that rode in splendour? Was it Death in radiant armour that passed from the room of death, with echoing footsteps clanking on stone stairs? Who brought the ghostly steed to the old porch of the House? Who carried the Banners before, which flowed and plunged in the mist? And whither, of your mercy, turns the Path of Souls which leads to the Bright Land under a Bright Sky? Is this the World of Faërie, or do we look for another?

Have you sat in such sorrowful, sad and haunted rooms as that where the Master passed? The ghosts of the old House held solemn vigil therein, watching by the dead in Faërie, yet they in mystic sleep. The great candles of the dead burnt in the place of mourning and the hallowed incense fumed, caught amidst the violet folds of a royal pall and its blazonry of crowns; for the dead Master came from a line of Kings, all dead and sheltered in the tomb. Their names and titles lived in Legends of the House, and the muniment room was full of their devices on banners. Prince Starbeam watched too, making offerings of will and the heart's purpose to the Court of Stars, praying to be led into Kinghood for the ends of the House and the rest of the Master's spirit. But not at this time or another could he find himself worthy, however he followed the quest, of the Throne and Crown of Faërie. The quest at least was his, and the call thereto; the next link in the chain would come in a due time, and that surely.

Have you heard the Call of Faërie?

Death is a veil in Faërie, and life is cloaked therein There came in its season the day for a Rite of the Dead, and with it came also watchers from many places, kinsmen of the old House, *videlicet*, princely strangers from countries far away and men from over the hills. The Keepers of old and the Clerks have sought in the muniment room, but they did not learn what voices and lights had led the mourners on, nor the place where the Master was laid. Yet is it very sure that the village priest who did the worshipful service in the name of the Houses of Heaven bequeathed a star to the stars. He said also: "The veils of night are dark, but the night is love." And yet again: "Behind the dark and the dole, a treasure of hidden gold." But after, at the very end: "The Star goes onward and onward: Lead us, O Star of Peace." When the service was over, one of the princely strangers, on behalf of them and of the kinsmen, approached and said to Prince Starbeam: "To the King in the day of his coming: unto you, our Prince, in Kinghood." And this speaker had the aspect of him who is true of voice in witness, even that Knight of the Swan in the BOOK OF THE VOICES OF FAËRIE, when he descended the Golden Stairs with a covenant from the Court of Stars. The watchers went upon their way, and thereafter, as he stood in the old porch, the ancient Usher approached and making obeisance said to Prince Starbeam: "Master of the House, they are spreading great news in the village: a spouse has been found for the Princess Cynthia, and this is Prince Melnor, son of the King of the Isle of Palms. He is said to have a Magic Ring, and to-morrow is the day of their betrothal."

The Gift of Brides in Faërie

Prince Starbeam answered, as one who speaks unawares: "O marriage of earth and Faërie;" and he was left deep in thought. He said at last, in colloquy with his own heart: "I will see this betrothal."

An orange sunset faded before him in the West: its last rays flushed his hair and forehead. The night fell; the moon rose: in distant thickets the nightingale poured forth her soul in song. Thereafter the night deepened, the wind heightened, and dark clouds scudded before the Queen of Heaven. Now and then there was soft patter of rain, and the last flowers in the ravaged garden gave forth fragrance of incense. Then it was very dark, till he was aware of divine eyes over against his own, how near and deeply speaking.

"Where the roads part by the woodland I gave a pledge," said the voice of the Beloved Kinsman.

The Wraith of a Pledge in Faërie

"It is in the heart of the beloved henceforward, to have and to hold," Prince Starbeam answered, and above the divine eyes there shone the crown of stars.

"I came out of the great distance, for your love's sake, as a brother."

"My life itself passed for the shaping of ends into the hands of another," and Prince Starbeam saw the face of the Beloved Kinsman, radiant against the veil of darkness.

"You gave unto me love for love."

"Till the asphodel moves the mountain;" and then Prince Starbeam saw the hands of the Beloved Kinsman as their fingers interlaced in his; but it seemed as an union of souls, beyond all welding of hearts.

"Link up your chain, my brother: I give you the next link; and then it shall lie in your hands for the doom of your life to forge till the way is short to the Kinghood. Because of the charge I gave you, the Magic Ring passed to the hand of another. I bid you remember this on the Day of Betrothal. When the woe of your days is with you, remember love for love. I am the Beloved Kinsman. In the presence of Prince Melnor and of her who rides beside, remember me."

"I see no longer a path but its thorns only."

"Before the crown of love is the crown of thorns."

A Mystery of Crowns in Faërie

For the Kisses of earth a moment, and peace in the heart which dreams upon them, saying: "Abide with me." For the Kisses of Faërie a moon hence, a year hence: perchance they are just beginning.

It was dark of dark in the night-time, and the Beloved Kinsman kissed Prince Starbeam, as it might be, a moment only, like one in haste to be gone. And the dawn blazed up in Faërie, red over earth and sea.

I have seen catafalques in Faërie and veiled forms thereon:
I bear my witness in Faërie that all death is figurative

XI

A DAY OF BETROTHAL IN FAËRIE

"I have been to the nuptials of Faërie, bearing my golden ring," says one of the Bridal Hymns. "I have wedded the World of Faërie, using the gage I bore. O place of many marriages." It was about noon when a long procession left the Temple in the chief city of the Golden Isles, where Prince Melnor and Princess Cynthia had been solemnly betrothed. Moreover the Lord Royal of the Golden Isles had proclaimed the Son of the Isle of Palms his heir and successor.

The Gift of Crowns in Faërie

The heart of the jewel is holy; there is health in the heart of the jewel; and fortified by the Magic Ring Prince Melnor reached the palace five days prior to the return of Prince Starbeam, when the custody of the old House in the waste and marish chase had passed on to another Keeper. Prince Melnor sought audience at once of the Lord Royal and shewing him the pearl beyond price of wonder laid claim upon another prize which it carried. It was not only compared most carefully with that of the Princess Cynthia and found to be a perfect counterpart, but those who were learned in the lore of stones, those who had wisdom in stellar workings and influence, and the Magus in chief who presided over a certain College of Magi testified to its star-origin. Thereupon the old monarch welcomed Prince Melnor with joy, saying that his heart had warmed towards him from the very beginning and that of all his daughter's suitors none had found such favour in his eyes. Moreover, he assured him of the speedy fulfilment of all his wishes. O caskets of wishes in

Faërie; but few are wise in the wishing, and this is the sorrow of Faërie. The return of her lover brought gladness to Princess Cynthia, so that glory and mercy were shining on every side; and whether or not there is no time to lose over marriages in Faërie, there was now at least no end in the zeal of the Lord Royal to speed the day of betrothal and open the nuptial gate so soon as the laws allowed. For the high office of nuptials in the Golden Isles made solemn betrothal precede the marriage rite.

The Marriage Crowns of Faërie

On this day therefore Prince Melnor ascended the first steps of his throne of bliss. Had he put aside all care and all dread of the morrow? Was the radiance of his outward aspect belied by gloom within? There was indeed a centre of darkness which put forth strange portents. How had he obtained the Magic Ring? He awoke to find it on his hand and Prince Starbeam was gone away—gone without telling his story, without a word of farewell, without accounting for his gift, if such indeed it were. Would he return and reclaim? Might not Prince Melnor himself have stolen the jewel in his sleep, in which case his deliverer would pursue and expose him? Was it credible that any one possessing that pearl without price should lightly transfer it to another? He could hope only that Prince Starbeam was after all a kind of ministering spirit, whom the Twelve Houses of Heaven had sent to his aid. But in the person of one of their messengers he had violated already an ordinance of the Court of Stars. Was he punished sufficiently for this in his long enchantment? And over and more than all, what was the threatened woe to follow his marriage union? In the face of this solemn warning from shapers of ends and dooms, the first rite of that union was now an accomplished fact, and he who had done nothing on his own part was betrothed to the Princess Cynthia and heir of the Golden Isles in virtue of that warrant which he wore indeed on his hand but had

O Place of many Captivities

not won. If guerdons earned by toil alone are truly ours, how long would these possessions remain to him? He looked about him, fearing to find an accuser in the cheering crowd, and his eyes fell on a white, despairing face. Pity him, Houses of Heaven: aid him, Court of Stars. Deathly seeming as it was, not he of all could mistake it. He knew his deliverer in a moment: that was the face of Prince Starbeam. But the cavalcade swept on, and he heard but could see no longer when an agonised cry rang out. Prince Starbeam had looked at last with his own eyes on the Princess Cynthia, of whom he had testified once that he had neither loved nor seen her. And the face of Princess Cynthia was that of his Dream-Lady, who had given him love for love in the Well of Vision.

Brides who were Queens' daughters have been given me in royal dreams:
But I am alone, and cold are the waters which wash before me and about

XII

THE MISSION FROM THE EVENING STAR

The beginning of stories in Faërie, beginning of light and joy; the lights and shadows of Faërie; the noon and the night therein; the woe and the weal thereof; the bitter cup and its drinking; the sword and the riven heart: But the end is always sure. And the Banners of Faërie float on the walls of Faërie, where still the vacant Throne awaits the Coming of the King.

With a loose rein, at the will of a faithful horse, grown old long since in the service of the old House, Prince Starbeam had ridden back to the waste and marish chase, nor knew how he reached his goal, for all faculties were dulled and all true sense suspended. The Usher of the House received him on the threshold of the House, in the old porch. Once and again the stars began to kindle over the sea, and Mars like a great cresset shone red in a sign of doom. The Usher was an ancient man, schooled in the ways of the House and especially in the rule of silence which reigned therein. He remembered also some part of its better days and he knew all its legends. I think in my heart that he knew of Prince Starbeam's quest and the woe of the Magic Ring. There were few servants below stairs in that broken day and he served the young Master himself in his patient preventing way with true loyalty of heart, alike at board and bed. In his great sorrow and stupefaction the Master blessed him with loving words, half-spoken on quivering lips; and in the deep sleep of his weariness the vision of Princess Cynthia shone through all his dreams.

Portents in Faërie

Records of the Past in Faërie

For the space of three days Prince Starbeam remained in the House, in the age-old book-room, among the muniments and archives, the old heirlooms and relics of an immemorial past. The ancient chests gave up their deeper secrets, and among them the true and faithful promises of HORON, the Star-Spirit, a genius of the House, to its traditional founder, King Leolyn. For many hours the young Master sat in the oriel window with that thin volume on his knees. The sunbeams fell on its quaint painted letters and broad, faded borders, full of symbolical pictures. They told of the Bright Land lying under the Bright Sky, the race and royalty of Faërie, the Rolls of Kinghood therein; and with a strange tincture of sentences they told also of the last cliff's end in Faërie, a great and breathless height, of the violet void beyond and then of a peopled vastness, as if out of time and place, the world of life for ever, far past all thought and vision.

On the second day of his tarrying a company of Seven Messengers, charged by the Evening Star as Herald of the Court of Stars to watch over the Magic Ring, appeared to Prince Starbeam and reproached him for giving to one selfish and unworthy that pure, many-virtued stone. They threatened the judgment of the Twelve Houses of Heaven on the profanation of the Mysteries of the Ring and brought him a solemn command to recover it. It was the next link in his chain, and he should go forth thereafter on Quest of the Beloved Kinsman. The Sons and Daughters of the Mystery come forth from the unknown and thither return unquestioned. Prince Starbeam listened and heard, but voice and the word failed him. He thought deeply in his heart that ways are long to the Kinghood and that he saw the path no longer but its thorns only. Hereof in the day of need is the working of alms in Faërie and what may bechance him who yieldeth stock and treasure. It must be said that the high spirit of the youth sank for a moment within him as the twilight darkened in the book-room. Strive as he might, the counsels and charges of him who was the Beloved Kinsman could not be brought into harmony with the present intervention direct from the Court of Stars and their Herald. By following the one he had lost to all appearance the Lady of his Life for ever, and under the new obedience he might lose the Brother of his Heart, to go on the quest of whom would therefore bring greater bitterness. Yet must he surely fulfil the ordination of the Evening Star. There was darkness within and without him. In the deep stress and the loneness he called on the Beloved Kinsman, but there was no answer, and no light of his coming. He passed along corridors and stairways, where the ghostly presences of the House fled at his approach, for the first time, as he thought. Looking up under the old porch, he saw over him the Evening Star, and because of it he was troubled and sorrowful in long dreams of the night.

Woe is me, O Faërie

But life and the triumph of life renewed its processions and pageants when again the morning flowed over; and the sun came up in the morning amidst the harps and organs of Nature. Acclamations and gladness of being called on the waking youth, and his heart answered with anthems. Behold also the Usher of the House—who had surely seen visions in sleep or heard a spirit of prophecy: he brought him fine and fair raiment out of fragrant presses of cedar and clothed him with his own hands. He knelt also before him and called him the King who was to come, paying homage on behalf of the House and in the name of all its Kindred. But Prince Starbeam raised him up with great worship, saying that, for himself, he was bidden on a long journey—as it seemed to him—very far away, and he covenanted the Usher of the House to keep the lamp burning, as a warning to ships at sea, for the sake of the good old custom and the saving honour of the

House. He gave him the Keys of the House and gave him also the stewardship, to have and to hold till the providence of the Court of Stars was known more fully concerning them. So he who was Usher and Steward pledged his faith before the Twelve Houses of Heaven.

Embassies of Faërie

But this was the third day, and through a village on a further side of the waste and marish chase there passed a mounted herald inquiring for him who was Prince Starbeam, because he was needed forthwith at the palace of the Lord Royal. He had travelled through twelve townships and twelve hamlets in the space of three days. Confusion of many voices and a great stir followed, for the old House in the Chase was a hold of mystery and wonder in the mind of the country-side. But the herald was in fine directed, and as one who prepares all things because he is forewarned of all, the Usher in fine received him with the immemorial courtesies and announced his presence to the Prince. The Records of the House have been questioned, to learn in what glass of vision he had seen the messenger on his road and read the purpose in his heart. It is known only that he had clothed his Master on the morning of this day as one who should go to a palace.

The Signs of Kinghood in Faërie

So the Herald was refreshed and being upstanding thereafter, Prince Starbeam entered and learned from his lips the will of the Lord Royal: that he should come forthwith to the Palace on the business of the Throne. He answered that he would do so gladly, for he also had business there which had been delayed too long already. When he was ready for that journey Prince Starbeam went apart with the Usher and charged him lovingly once more, as one who was henceforward the Steward of the House and its Mystery, to keep the lamp burning and to guard the sacred archives till the day of his return, or him failing the rightful heir carrying the proper warrants. The ancient man swore to be faithful and true. Prince Starbeam blessed him on the part of the House and on his own part with the Kiss of Peace in the House. And the Usher answered on his knees: " To you, my Prince, in Kinghood," for he knew the lore of the House. By this time the horses were ready, and they rode off in the sunlight. At the end of seven hours they saw the great towers of the Palace looming in the mist of distance.

Who rides and draws not Rein ?

Up in the air and down in the sea, over the hills and away;
But ever the voice of comfort breathes between the sedges,
Ever behind the hedges: it sings far up in the heights,
And its lullaby is here in the hollows

XIII
THE OBSCURE NIGHT OF FAËRIE

The priests of those mysteries offered up the Sun in sacrifice on the altar of the western edge. When the guests of the high festival departed in fine from the Palace it was late night, and Prince Melnor went out into the lonely, fragrant grounds—to still, if that were possible, a nameless dread at his heart. A thousand times he asked himself what meant Prince Starbeam's presence in the crowd and was that his voice which cried?

The suspense of these unanswerable questions still tortured him when there came at his side a sudden voice of warning and voice of high proclamation. Behold now, he stood again in the presence of that Wise Master who was the Hermit of his first quest. The hush of the darkness intimates deeper things than speech, and its silent rumours were about him before he spoke.

The Wind of the Spirit in Faërie

"I am sent to you for the last time," he said. "Remember your faithless ways, by which you have brought wretchedness and ruin on your parents. This you can never repair; but it is not too late to withdraw from your present course, wherein is the harvest to come of your own misery. Give unto me that Magic Ring, of which you are unworthy. Leave this Palace privately and never return hereto, nor to the presence of Princess Cynthia. Such is the way of safety."

"You bid me renounce all my hopes of happiness," cried the distracted Prince. "You bid me forego the seal of youth and beauty. You bid me leave the Lady of my love, her who is now my consort. What woe can be greater than such a sacrifice ? Explain its nature, and let me judge for myself."

"The Stars have spoken," answered the Wise Master. "The Voice of the Stars ordains. This warning is given you that in the day of your undoing you may have no one to accuse but yourself."

He stepped back in the speaking, with hands upraised, and the gesture seemed to Prince Melnor as though he had been cast out by the Court of Stars, or that a malediction had been pronounced upon him by Twelve Houses of Heaven.

As a pillar of ice, the infatuated Prince remained fixed in the dread of his thought; and then Voices of Faërie, Voices over land and water. There appeared the seven bright spirits who are guardians of a Magic Ring—Children of Election in Faërie, Sons of Desire, Daughters of the Golden Voice. They pleaded with him in the Voice of Faërie; they adjured him to renounce the Magic Ring. In a frenzy, Prince Melnor dashed himself to the ground and that vision dissolved in music. The tears that are idle in Faërie are tears of hate, and they scorched his eyes as they fell. As the night air revived him he rose to his feet and cried through his set teeth: "I will not give in. I will go on to the bitter end. I will conquer Fate."

Of Preaching to Spirits in Prison

He fled towards the Palace. A stranger of stately mien, and bearing on his breast one of the greater sigils of the Court of Stars, met him almost on the threshold and said in a cold voice, apart from all severity, as it might be a grave speaking: "I have a mission to the Prince Melnor: His parents are dead, his city is in ruins, they perished in exile." With no other word of reproach, he stepped back and was received by the darkness.

O espousals of Faërie, where even the beasts of the field come in their wedding garments. Within the Palace itself the distracted Prince was met presently by the Lord Royal,

The Price of a Path in Faërie

who rallied him blithely on his absence and then embraced him, saying how gladly he should entrust to his care the life and joy of his daughter. Safe in his arms and shielded she might rest surely because he had won the Magic Ring, and he gave the reason why. There had come on a day to the Palace a certain worshipful stranger who spoke to him darkly in secret concerning talismans of flowers, of secrets hidden in flowers and flowers that speak in the heart. " I remember him as an ancient man when he began recounting his legend," said the Lord Royal, " and he drew me to open my heart, which was ever on the quest of a Prince with a Magic Ring. But he looked now in his majesty like one of the Wise Masters or a Messenger from the Court of Stars. As those who have power, alike in word and deed, he spoke also with majesty, pleading in the name of his mission and of the Twelve Houses of Heaven. He bade me beware of him, were he prince or peasant, who had given false troth in Faërie and found the doom of its keeping at the hands of a Queen of Roses. The Magic Ring could preserve in perpetuity the youth and beauty of Cynthia, but in such case it would not preserve her from death on the bridal night. The Messenger said, moreover, that one who had kept and cherished the dower of a Queen of Roses could never by his own effort obtain the Magic Ring."

The bewrayed Prince had opened many doors in Faërie, and they were doors which looked towards self; but now at long last he was overwhelmed, if not indeed subdued. He staggered and fell swooning to the floor. It was near midnight, the tired pages were at rest. The Lord Royal stood staring, with clasped hands, at the prostrate form, whose face shone white in the rays of a distant lamp. He uttered a cry which summoned the drowsy warders, but or ever they heard and came there were rumours and movements, as of beings and things unseen. Of a truth

The House is walking in its Sleep

there are many witnesses in those old palaces of Faërie, its precincts and its thresholds. The Prince was borne into one of the banqueting halls, and while means were taken to restore him, the Lord Royal was seeking to account for the effect produced by his brief recital. He at least had noticed a sudden and deathly change which came over the face of Melnor as the pageant swept back from the Minster. He had seen also the agonised countenance of an unknown youth in the crowd and heard his cry ring out. A misgiving entered his mind. He had heard but a vague tale of finding the Magic Ring. What if he had been deceived? What if—after all—it were only a clever counterfeit? A College of Magic might err and so also the lapidaries.

While these problems perplexed him, the Prince revived and sat up with wild eyes. The Lord Royal approached him and dismissed the attendants. There were questions and counter-questions. A little help is worth a world in Faërie: who should help them now? The prize of beauty in Faërie is a high prize at the end of a long journey. Moreover, the great things are earned and not given. This is a truth which is either found in action or taught in bitterness. Prince Melnor was learning it now. That which the warnings and counsel of the Wise Master, the dole of his parents, pleadings of Guardian Spirits and forecasts of his own dole to come could in no wise compass was achieved by the danger of Cynthia, and now from beginning to end he told his whole story. Though assured in respect of the Ring, the Lord Royal was deep in wrath and distress. His long deferred hope had suffered crushing defeat on the very threshold of fulfilment. There was every blame attaching to Prince Melnor, save in the gift of the Ring, for he knew nothing of its story; but he saw that the greater dispraise rested here on himself, who had hurried the espousals without citing the conditions. Prince Melnor, on his own part, had not paltered with the truth, in so far

Of Shadows cast in Faërie

as he knew it, when he said that one who was unknown had dissolved his long enchantment and given him the Ring in his sleep.

Meanwhile, the illness of her betrothed was news that travelled, and presently it reached the Princess, who came down into the great hall, a train of maidens following. Her solicitude and unlooked for presence dismayed them further. Prince Melnor broke in tears because she was lost to him for ever. He had otherwise the aspect of a man overwhelmed by sudden catastrophe, while the Lord Royal was strangely beside himself. With words of sweetness she sought to restore her lover, to still her father's trouble with words of peace. But these things profited nothing. Of what had befallen she asked on her own part, and as one whose caution forsakes him the Lord Royal led her presently aside. Out of her heart of goodness, for them and for her, he bade her remember the warning of that Wise Master, Messenger from the Court of Stars, and said that she could not accept the Prince as her spouse without setting it at nought. The Prince was ill indeed, but it was because he had proved unworthy. The Magic Ring which should have been his guarantee and her safeguard had been given him and not won: he had indeed done nothing to deserve it.

Coin of Kindness: Current Coin of Faërie

The Princess did not swoon or shed tears, and at a sign from the Lord Royal she suffered her women to lead her away. Prince Melnor saw her depart: in truth she passed by him as one unaware of his presence. Full of agony, his eyes followed her and then turned mutely to her father. But the old man sat down at the foot of the couch, his hands clasped on his knees, his head bowed forward. The Prince, raised on one elbow, looked vacantly at him and no words were spoken. One after another the lamps in the hall went out: it was dark night in the Palace. It seemed to Prince Melnor in his misery that he had made void the

Magic Ring, or that its virtue had turned to rend him. The arrow flying in the day is blunted by the shield of Faërie; the business haunting the darkness is disarmed therein; the noonday demon is turned aside and bound. But these are salvations reserved for the true of heart. It was dark of dark in the Palace, and clocks striking the hours uttered words of doom. But those hours wore on. A faint grey glimmer began to filter through vast windows eastward: the deep night lifting shewed fields and forests folded in thin veils of mist. The light restores the vision within as well as without, and the Lord Royal lifted his head as the sun rose, for light had dawned in his mind. But the Prince buried his face in the silken cushions of the couch when he saw the glory of morning, and his eyes would not meet it, till presently a stir of life beginning to be heard in the Palace, and he crept to his own rooms.

New Thought in the Morning

The hopes of the Lord Royal revived at the sudden thought of that strange youth who had given the Ring to Prince Melnor and had been seen in the crowded street as the late pageant passed through. He might not be beyond reach. The Lord Royal resolved on his quest and his finding. He would then dissolve a betrothal which was now without meaning, since the two contracting parties had been separated by the Court of Stars and set apart for ever. He would persuade or compel Melnor to restore the Magic Ring to its first owner, who should then marry his daughter and so fulfil his now frustrated purpose. In the first place he had recourse to the College of Magic, as it was necessary to learn the name of the strange youth. It was a great office of records, of many chronicles and digests, but these did not help him. It was a place of many processes in time-old magical arts, nativities, portents and auguries, over which it proceeded according to traditional methods and was prone to get lost therein. It was not a

World without End in Faërie

very wise place, though it demanded much worship and claimed very high titles, so it was only in the last resource that the question was referred to the vestals and they divined thereon in consecrated glasses of vision. The face and aspect of Prince Melnor being known to all in the College because of the betrothal could be brought easily into the crystal globes, but it was difficult to isolate him from Beryl, the Queen of Spells, who predominated everywhere in his atmosphere. When they had conjured her out of the glasses, the Princess Cynthia appeared, a fair shadow beheld as from a great distance. She went of her own accord, and it was then only that some of the vestals saw Prince Starbeam in their vision, amidst a glory from the Magic Ring. They proclaimed him of royal race, but of his story they learned nothing, for the high election of a Court of Stars is hidden from a College of Magic. He seemed to come nearer within their range of vision in the street crowd of the pageant, being the great day of his sorrow. Even then it was she only of all most pure and fair, who was able to read his name. She read it twice over and twice in a different sense—once as the King who is to come and once as Prince Starbeam. There was joy in the College of Magic, and the Lord Royal read in the first title a promise which crowned his hopes.

Beauty is Magic in Faërie

With such hopes in his heart he sought out Princess Cynthia, whom he found in her own chamber, seated in the great embayed window, with her women—who were seven radiant maidens. These were weeping, but the Princess was pale, and very calm in her silence. He motioned the maidens away and taking her cold hand, asked how it was with her. She answered: "Sir, it is well with me no more while I wear a Magic Ring. Great gifts bring with them great sorrows: it has been thus, both to thee and to me."

"Let us wait a little," said the Lord Royal. "That

which has come into my mind may yet help us. Keep therefore the Magic Ring."

He rose and went from her. But she watched by the window till evening.

"What will you do?" said the Lord Royal to Prince Melnor, when messengers had been despatched far and wide through the Golden Isles to find Prince Starbeam and bring him with speed to the Palace. "You are betrothed in words only, which now have no meaning."

The Prince answered: "My father and mother are dead; the Kingdom has passed from my hands. All things turn for me to evil: let us wait a little. My deliverer was present in the crowd on the day of my life in Faërie. If I may find him, he will surely help and heal me these wounds of life."

Coming of Saviours in Faërie

O way of the world in Faërie, beyond the aching days. The dead hours dropped slowly from the Tree of Time. In the evening the Princess went down alone into the great hall. The moonlight streamed through the windows —moon of the World of Faërie. Prince Melnor sat at a long table of carven oak, his face hidden in his hands. He started, looked up and rose with a low cry. Together they passed into the deep recess of an oriel window and sat down without speaking in high-backed chairs. The clock goes forward in Faërie, the clock goes back, and there are spaces between some moments when no clock moves at all. Life and time, time and life--how still they stood in the stillness. But the tears of love-lies-bleeding are tears of pearls, and such was the mourning of Cynthia. She had heard the whole story from other lips than his—was this in a dream of the night?—and she knew how such stories end. Now love had bled to death and lay upon the trestles. But O the pity of heart in Faërie, fondness of broken hearts. There are no words because of it, and yet the spirit ministers. So did the balm of her presence fall on his open

Waiting and Watching in Faërie

wounds. The ascending moon grew brighter, its beams brooded in a halo round their heads, and the Rings which they wore shone strangely. It was near midnight when she rose up in her beauty and gave him hands of benediction in the quivering hands of him, saying: "To you at the end in peace." And he who had been broken answered: "The end is you. I have lost my end in Faërie."

When birds sang in Faërie, then I took heart of grace:
The days pass, the years pass; the Swan and its songs are with me

XIV

HAND AND CROWN IN FAËRIE

A rose on the pillow in Faërie, a rose of dreams; a rose of joy on the pillow, a rose of light; a rose which closes its petals, a rose of death; and roses of vision in Faërie, faces within the vision, in strange castles of sleep. Out of a haunted sleep the Princess rose in the morning. She had prayed to the face in her vision and called thereon—an old, familiar face in moons of dream. There is borne true witness that Faërie is the bodying forth of the ideal, and the inward goodness moulds the outward form. Perchance it was over the borders, over the sea of clouds; but the face which had brought her the blessing in other days than these, and the worshipful, sacred eyes had spoken peace in the silence. She awakened as one who is consoled.

Faces of Vision in Faërie

It was the third day after his messengers started, and the hope of the Lord Royal was failing. Prince Melnor sat stricken, for the most part in solitude. It was late in the afternoon when the light turned amber and golden; there was a sense of unseen presences, a scent of the beanfields of Faërie, and a new heart of meaning in the life of things. As one who feels suddenly that he is standing on the threshold of events, the Lord Royal took his seat of state in the great throne-room of the Palace, with his daughter and Prince Melnor on one and the other side. The jewelled doors of the chamber were opened wide, and through vestibules beyond they could see that other doors were also thrown back. The broad vistas of the park and innumerable purple hills had taken on strange vestures in the unwonted splendour of light. And the splendour flowed into the throne-room. The Lord Royal contemplated in the light and was amazed.

A Pageant of Faërie

After a little space there appeared suddenly, as on either side of the door and within the threshold, two golden horns of Faërie, of great length and beautiful; but the bearers were not seen, save for their white hands, wearing rings of profession. These horns of proclamation were sounded sweetly and strangely; they were like horns over waters, at first heard from far away, but coming nearer and ever nearer, till their torrents of melody crashed against walls and ceiling. "I have heard such music in my heart on a day of my Lady which is marked double in the rubrics," it is said on the margin of one of the old rolls, "so I know that the quest is true and its crown certain, Amen, world without end for ever." In the silence which followed, a voice—like a royalty of the spirit heralded in a Kingdom of the Blessed—chanted or sang thus, as if on one side, over the northern horn, since the Throne looked to the West:

V. I hear thy voice in the rivers, thy face is behind the trees.

And then another voice, which was like good things known in the heart, made answer on the southern side:

R. Wherever the sun shines, there is the light of thine eyes.

The challenge and responsion continued:

V. Thy picture is borne in procession, but where is he who is imaged?

R. Many are brought in thy likeness: not thou, not thou art there.

V. The heart tires in the quest.

R. Each moon looks nearer and nearer, yet art thou far away.

V. I have sought through the highlands and islands, the forests and fells, city and wilderness.

R. Has this world only his picture, or kindred fair of face?

V. Each quest leads me further.

R. I have been to the world's verge and the home of souls.

V. Is he hidden in the soul of things?

R. Has earth opened to hide him or deep of sea received?

V. Turn again, tides of ocean.

R. Turn, O earth again.

There was then a space of silence, save the breath of the breezes of Faërie, like flute-notes without the palace. And now, finally, there came a voice of majesty, the power of a royal anthem, as in a place beyond the threshold; but this said in its nobility: "I have seen the King in his beauty: in a dream of the heart I saw him." And so, even as they came, those mellow horns of Faërie were taken out of the way.

True of Voice in Faërie

The Lord Royal sat on his jewelled Throne, and the words of wonder, words that came to his lips, were cut off in the heart. Prince Melnor rose panting, as one who —beyond expectation—looks for deliverance at hand. But the Princess Cynthia stood up with clasped hands, saying within herself: "My vision is to me, and unto my vision am I"—as one who utters in the spirit divine words: *Quia tuus sum ego.* But now the ushers of the Court Royal on the further side of the portal announced the coming of the Prince—to wit, Prince Starbeam, of the race and royalty of Leolyn, by election of the Court of Stars. Some have searched all the records and have not learned by whom these words of grace were put into the mouth of speakers who were servants in a King's Palace. But there is a memorial in one of the transcripts which says that the Court of Stars did honour to him who was elected on the threshold of the King's Palace, and others have

Love in the House of Kindness

found herein an allusion to this pageant. Of a truth the Twelve Houses of Heaven are Houses and Heavens of love.

And Prince Starbeam entered, who at that time was of age about eighteen summers, and looked as he looks only who is heir of promises reserved in a Bright Land lying under a Bright Sky; who has been borne over a sea of cloud into the Land of Faërie; who has been kissed by its Queen-Royal; who has worshipped with a Daughter of the Stars; and has worn—be it ever so briefly—a Magic Ring formed under high influences of an Evening Star. He was one in whom stars took flesh, to justify his name and election—out of thousands—by Twelve Houses of Heaven. If his eyes were a House of Heaven, it will be understood that he was beautiful by all measures of dream in Faërie; and for some who have dwelt in contemplation where his statues may be seen on the borders in places within the freedom, he was himself a world of Faërie. Withal he looked—as it seemed to those who beheld him—passing young—notwithstanding the high erected bearing of his modesty. It is not known how the Lord Royal received him, save that at this time he was gracious who afterwards turned against him. Prince Melnor remembered and was glad for the first time since the doom of the Ring was told him. But though the Princess Cynthia stood, it was as one who could have knelt, in worship of heart and soul, for his was the face of her vision, as hers was the face of his love. During certain moons it had been with her, and peradventure at those moments when he beheld her gracious wonder in that woodland well, she had looked also on him. But he had been with her in dreams of the night, and she on her part had given him love for love, save that in her it was at that time a love of the spirit—as it might be, a maid's devotion to an angel-guide. So was it therefore with marvel and a certain high dread of heart that she saw him now, clothed with the vesture of humanity.

The Mind of Faërie

He was to her as the denizen of a star or an abider in the heart of Faërie.

Because I love you, is Faërie

But what was it now unto him, as he stood in her presence, knowing nothing of that which had passed in the last days, holding her only the betrothed Lady of one unto whom he had given—at another's bidding—that palladium of a Magic Ring? He knelt before the Lord Royal and was raised; he greeted Prince Melnor with words of friendship; to the Princess Cynthia he offered silent homage, with bowed head. And the great debate began. He was questioned by the Lord Royal respecting his race and its royalty, and the land from which he derived. He was questioned concerning the Magic Ring and how it came into his hands. He told of his father's ordinance and that which followed in quest, but not of the Golden Stairs and not of the Throne in Faërie, nor yet the secret of his heart in the Haunted Well. The spirit of the Lord Royal beat high within him, for it seemed to him surely that the valiant and beautiful youth was predestined by the Court of Stars to claim a Bride and Throne. "On the highlands and the lowlands, on sea and land, I have been looking for him all my life," thought the Lord Royal; and it came to him that he might be at peace henceforward in his age, where the asp does not come, nor the basilisk, and the lion and the dragon are on the other side of the world.

Moonset at Parting

It came about therefore that his manner of speaking was kind as a father's welcome when he asked the one question that was nearest of all to his hopes. At the very beginning thereof, the Princess Cynthia, divining that which was to come, rose up and left the Throne Room. Prince Starbeam thought in his heart: "It is thou in the world of Faërie, ever and only thou." The question was whether Prince Starbeam went on his quest of the Magic Ring because of the reward attached to it or because of his father's ordinance. The Prince answered that it was to link up a chain of life.

Had he ever seen the Princess? the Lord Royal asked. He had seen her in sacred vision, of which he must forbear to speak. The heart of the King gave a leap within him, as if he saw Fate moving to the right hand of his hope. Why was Prince Starbeam stricken and what meant that wailing cry which he uttered in the midst of the pageant? The face of the Prince whitened and his eyes shone: It was then only he knew that Princess Cynthia was his high Lady of Vision. Who was the Beloved Kinsman? But earth and sea could not answer, so far as Prince Starbeam knew. Why was he told to renounce the Magic Ring after its quest was crowned? It was because of another link in a chain of life. Did it signify that Prince Melnor was destined to wed the Princess and to keep the Magic Ring? Reluctant and yet relieved that a path had opened direct to his painful mission, Prince Starbeam answered that the Twelve Houses of Heaven had over-ruled the ordinance of the Beloved Kinsman, who was perhaps the genius of his House, and he had received a counter-mandate from Seven Messengers charged by the Evening Star to take back the jewel. He held out his hands to Prince Melnor and said: "I ringed you in your sleep, my Brother, and that which I gave was given, regretting nothing and making no claim on you. In what I am now bidden the act is not on my part. Had I known that the Princess Cynthia was my well-beloved Lady of Vision I should have obeyed the behest still and linked up my chain of life, however heavy the links. It would have been done in sorrow then; and now that I am here in the name of a new purpose, still is the part not mine, nor the Ring to be called my own. For I go on another mission and do not see my end. I await a further mandate in respect of the Ring."

Guardians of the Ring

There was silence in the Palace—as it seemed, for a long space. Again the voices of those who were invisible sounded at the far end of the Throne Room, each unto each responding :

V. Thou art the end of things, O Faërie, the immemorial mode.

R. The meditations are thine and the dreams are thine also.

V. I have contemplated in the heart with thee.

R. I have seen in thy glass of vision.

V. I have been on the borders of Faërie, but who has been to the heart ?

R. The pilgrim said : I was there : it is the place of the keeping of love.

These voices ceased, and the wonder in the heart of Prince Starbeam was greater than the King's wonder. Prince Melnor thereupon took the Ring from his hand and knelt before his deliverer of old, saying : "You ringed me in sleep, my Saviour, but you will I ring in my waking ;" and so doing it was the first act which was accounted unto him for blessedness.

I have paid the Price of my Reckoning

"The Stars have you in their holy keeping, and the Daughter of the Stars be with you," said Prince Starbeam. But to the Lord Royal he said that the Ring should be put into a casket in the Minster attached to the Palace on the High Altar of the Stars, until the Seven Messengers should direct him further concerning it. And this having been done presently, a light was set burning before it and seven maidens, vested in white, bearing each of them a golden censer, were put to guard it.

There arose now the last question of the time, and this was whether Prince Melnor could yet do anything by which he might deserve the Ring, that those who were lovers should be made one by love, in the place of its keeping. It was asked by Prince Melnor himself, and the Lord Royal had no joy therein, for his desire had turned to him who had been chosen out of many by the Court of Stars.

In this manner Prince Starbeam learned the doom attached to the Ring, though there was little profit to the teller, since he who had finished his quest of the Magic Ring knew not the Mystery of Roses. But when he had thought a little in the silence, he said—as it might be, looking through a glass of vision: "In my heart I believe that she who is Queen of Roses and Spells has not yet finished her dealings and that you will yet be brought together. But I think in the end that a path may open beyond the Spells and Roses into places of peace and the light of your work in Faërie."

The Mirror of Faërie

At the same moment a melancholy, long-drawn wail arose in the space between them, and they were aware of a shadowy presence, very dim by the side of Prince Melnor, as if it were a Queen of Roses in the red of her fatal sacraments, exhaling the scent thereof. O savour and odour of spices, filling the heart with sweetness. But Prince Melnor shrank in fear, dreaming of other enchantments, and the presence faded as it came, lamenting.

Afterwards the Lord Royal spoke apart with Prince Starbeam, saying that his daughter's espousals were about to be annulled, since any union was impossible between the two contracting parties. He exhorted the Prince to take back the Magic Ring, offering the hand of the Princess, with the crown of the Kingdom as his heirship, on that condition. O heart of life in Faërie, O heart of life. Was it not the hardest, if not the last ordeal for that son of the House of Leolyn? Have you followed your star in Faërie? Tell me where it has led, through the dark and the light ways. Prince Starbeam called upon the Court of Stars, who had doubtless fixed her image in that Haunted Well, to witness that its sacred picture was the life of his life in Faërie, and in all the world beside. But he was bidden on a journey which might take him far and away, while the issues of this event were in other hands than his.

The Tree of Life in Faërie

What was the reason and purpose of that journey? the Lord Royal asked. Prince Starbeam answered that it was a Quest of the Beloved Kinsman, and he had learned too well in his travels that the way is long to Kingship. This Quest had been imposed by those same Seven Messengers who were Heralds of the Evening Star.

But these workings vexed the patience of the Lord Royal no less than they confused his reason; and he shewed himself more than disposed to regard that mysterious Kinsman as a maker of strife in Faërie, who worked counter to the Stars. Prince Starbeam was faithful and true, so he held that later events would loosen all tangled skeins. Meanwhile he desired above all to have audience of Princess Cynthia, because there were things reserved for her ears alone. He prayed therefore for this great boon. It is very sure that the Lord Royal misliked all secret dealings, because he was a great King who should not be denied knowledge of that which took place in his islands, but especially in his own palace. Still he made grace of the granting, for it might somehow turn to his profit. In the moon of his daughter's beauty there was much to be hoped also for one who was tried hardly between love and a quest in dark.

The Wish and the Will in Faërie

But Prince Starbeam must sit first at the board of the Lord Royal, for the hour had come, and moreover his guest had journeyed. So they sat at table together, and Prince Melnor was third in the conclave. But concerning this bond of bread and salt in the Palace of the Golden Isles there is not found a record. The law over trifles in Faërie is perchance a law of silence.

The law of trifles in Faërie is a law of mustard-seed, and great are the growths therefrom

XV

THE WAY OF A CROWN IN FAËRIE

"I loved good things from the beginning: I sought them the whole world over, in and out of the years; but nothing kept of all. I found on a day in Faërie that the one good thing is love. Love is the signet-ring, and love is the seal of all. Love is the act and deed which delivers the lesser goods and the greater. Love is the tingeing stone. Shine upon me, Stars of Faërie. Love is my title and love my warrant in the Quest of the Great King." So opens a Tale of Quest, the Quest and Way of a Crown.

O Mastery and Alchemy

Prince Starbeam was ushered by Heralds of the King's Palace into the presence of Princess Cynthia. She rose in her beauty to greet him, like a Moon of the Spirit which shines for a season in a place of material things. The gifts of Faërie are not gifts of the Spirit. They are rather from the soul of things and lights for the lost therein. But the two who stood now together had dowers from a higher region, even the Court of Stars: they had heard of an Everlasting King, Who is the beginning and end of Kingship, there where no man has travelled, above the Court of Stars. Of a truth there are many hierarchies, or the woods and the waters of Faërie, the waters and woods without, were not so full of dwellers. Also the sea has its palaces, and the dome of heaven is not an empty dome.

Those twain sat down together and—outside the life of vision—they made a first study in the secrets of joy and immortality within each other's eyes. For Prince Starbeam it was looking more deeply into eyes of the Haunted Well, and they gave him love for love in the deep within their

Lamps of Faërie

deep, far past the body of things. For the Princess Cynthia it seemed more and more that spirit made answer to spirit, that she loved and worshipped then, beyond the simple inclinations of the lower heart of flesh. Of such is the opening of souls in Faërie: Who reads in the open soul? It came about therefore that no words of love were exchanged at this time between them. But Prince Starbeam the whole structure of his life shewed to the Princess Cynthia, that she might know the end of his House and his own ends—*videlicet:*

(1) The hope of his House, to return thither whence they had come at first, being that Pure Land lying under a Pure Sky, which his honourable and loving father had revealed to him at the time of his passing as the Blessed Land and the Blessed Life of Faërie;

(2) The BOOK OF TRUE VOICES, the QUEST OF THE GOLDEN STAIRS and the hope of his heart therein;

(3) How he had been unawares into Faërie and found that the BOOK OF TRUE VOICES was a Book of Truth in the Art, for the Throne indeed was vacant;

(4) How voices of Faërie and others yet, on the hither side of the threshold, had hailed him as a King who was to come;

(5) How it might so be perchance that the fortune of his House awaited restoration in him, and that—albeit one who was unworthy—he was keeping sacred in his heart a dream of the Kingdom in Faërie.

A Secret kept by Stars

Were all this true, he said that he should understand better that Quest of the Beloved Kinsman on which he was now sent out into the world. He had seen the Kinsman in his glory: perchance he was the Genius of the House. But whether the Magic Ring was a title of Kinghood in Faërie or something to be gained on the way and then renounced he did not know, and this was why it had been set on the High Altar of the Stars until he should learn further. But a light of the eyes might dawn, did he hear—as he hoped—how the Ring had come to her, the Royal Lady of the Golden Isles.

Over and over the Princess Cynthia had been saying in her own soul: The aspiration of Faërie is: Make me in the likeness of the Highest. And he who sat with her, telling his tale of wonder, looked highest of all in her dream. But she said in answer: "O chosen Prince of Faërie, it is mine to wait with you. In a hidden close of the gardens about this palace there came a Messenger on the part of the Court of Stars, who decreed the Ring as a dower, to have and to hold thenceforth, awaiting a day to come when their will should be known further." She told him also in her purity that it was a gage for the day of her marriage, but a blot had come on that scutcheon and she would fain put aside the Ring till the Stars decreed concerning it. Prince Starbeam could say only that he had renounced his own by an ordinance and could only reclaim by one.

Love is the Legal Tender

The Princess Cynthia arose and he also. The gauze of her garments was like gauze out of moonbeams woven. She gave him both her hands, and said: "We have known one another, my Prince, in a different dream of life and were pledged to each other therein, as a soul is pledged to its star. I know not where we shall meet or when in the coming time, but it is not henceforth in vision—perchance at the top of the Golden Stairs when the way is short to the Kinghood."

"On the threshold of Kinghood, where two shall be found as one," Prince Starbeam answered. "Thou also knowest, O High Lady of Life. The Stars are only beginning their work in thee and in me. But thou art my Lady, and I am thy Prince in service."

Their eyes met, like planets of grace in conjunction. In the silence which followed a breath went by, as wind of the spirit in Faërie—a breathing, a music, and then a voice of rapture. It sang of one thing only which I have been looking for all my life.

"O Priestess of Faërie, where Priesthood is beauty and beauty is grace of soul:
Thy seven vestures of beauty are raised by the Rites of thy Priesthood.
The lifting of each veil reveals a greater beauty.
After the last veil, it is known to be thou and no other.
The heart has waited long."

The Veil of Faërie

Hereof is the truth of Stars, and that vesture which is its nimbus. It is prophesied that Faërie will fold up its dream like a carpet of beautiful flowers, but of that which cometh thereafter, ask ye not now. For those twain there came a space of silence, and then Princess Cynthia said: "Ships shall not fail thee to sail the seas of vision, nor coaches and steeds on shore."

And he, as their hands loosened: "I have been in the House of Dreams: for a life, a life and a hundred lives I have dreamed in the House of Dreams. Thou art the end of my dreaming and the path that leads me home. Thou art the place of awakening, and the land that I left is nigh."

These were their words at parting.

Prince Starbeam said afterwards to the Lord Royal: "By thy grace, I will watch in the Minster: I look for news in the night."

"The peace of the Stars be with thee," answered the Lord Royal. "What of the Princess Cynthia?"

"I see the path opening and a crown at the end thereof."

"Be therefore my son," said the monarch. "My life grows weary in waiting and my end is nigh."

"My desire is to the honour of thy house, and thy joy were mine."

The Lord Royal embraced him, and Prince Starbeam went up alone to the Minster, relieving the vigil of maidens with the immemorial courtesies of those who remember the Bright Land lying under a Bright Sky amidst the wastes and solitudes of a marish chase.

Of wishing-gates in Faerie and the world beyond

XVI

A PRIEST OF STARS

O House of perfect silence: the air was still and sacred in the great Minster, and the Magic Ring shone with its native light. The flowers on the Altar had more than their own lustre and seemed changing, like that Agnus Castus which its presence had immortalised when the Invocation of the Daughter of the Stars brought down the jewel of life. Of words of grace and power which are spoken in the Language of the Stars Prince Starbeam as yet knew nothing; but the Litanies of his own House remained in his memory and he recited them now on his knees before the High Altar. He remembered a Mystic Service in the Chapel of the wild old chase—as it might be, a Mass of the Stars—in far-off days, when the House had fallen indeed, but some of its state remained. It is known that there are Missals everywhere, and a Gothic Mass-Book may open the World of Faërie. It opened in Prince Starbeam's heart, as there he knelt in contemplation, the heart stilling within him. And presently the one image of his life was present in its pure shining, and the light of her eyes was like the light of a Magic Ring. The painted windows of the Minster were filled with living figures. There arose in the midst of his dreaming, very softly and sweetly, the voices of a choir invisible—as it seemed to him—behind the Altar, intoning strange, true things concerning the Quest and its very worshipful end, concerning the Life of Faërie and the paths that lead beyond. Peradventure the versicles came to him in fragments only, or perchance he lost some of them, because of the image in his heart. There is a light

Illuminated Missals of Faërie

of pure shining which at times suspends remembrance. "I have followed the flight of a doe through forests, and far between old hills," says one of the Master-Songs. "A star shines on its forehead, leading through dark ways and the nights therein. And somewhere—somewhere—at the end of the doe's flight, is the maid of my world of dreams, who awaits my coming. Was not the doe herself my Atalanta flying? But I lost both star and doe because of the one image, in thoughts of the heart thereon."

A little Light shall lead them

The voices said in their chanting: "Drape me a shining veil, and I will take unto me a crescent Moon, and will move as a pilgrim in Faërie."

And thereafter: "A road which leads to Faërie, a white and winding road; a road which goes through Faërie and out at the further side, in another place of the world. Whither, O whither? But who of all shall say?"

And then again, as if ringing the changes: "A bye-lane, a narrow lane, a very crooked path, a track over green meadows, a path beside the brook. But this is the way into Faërie, and this goes also through."

Give me the Freedom of Faërie

Afterwards, over and over: "I have come out of Faërie, and its odours cling to my garments."

Then, with a pause between: "I have heard all the rumours; I have listened to all the voices; I have seen the great pageants: where is the peace of thy silence, beyond the dream and the vision?"

And so in the last place, like unto a bell for clearness: "Where is thy World of Spirit?"

He was even a Priest of the Stars who ascended the steps of the Altar and opened that crystal casket. It was even a Priest of the Stars who took out the Magic Ring and turning faced Prince Starbeam. But he looked like that Master in Chief of the Portal, whose faithful testimony is recorded in the SWORN BOOK OF THE VOICES OF FAËRIE. It was even a Priest of the Stars who ringed Prince Starbeam on his knees; but he had the aspect of a Keeper of the Precincts, of him who is true of voice, and he had eyes that the heart has not fathomed, like those of the Beloved Kinsman. He closed the hand of the Prince over the radiant jewel and said: "A Ring of Profession in Quest, to have and to hold for a season, devise and find again, to suffer the weird thereof, to be strong and to win through. A new link in the chain, and yet a link shall follow: then is it near the end. Hereof is the way of the Kinghood and the way that leads to thy marriage above the Golden Stairs."

In that moment Prince Starbeam knew certainly for the first time that the end of his Quest was indeed the Crown of Faërie and that the Princess Cynthia was his Bride to come. He knew also that there are higher consecrations than those of Faërie and that therefore his titles and warrants would come from the Court of Stars. . . . "I won my bride in a night, with the help of Faërie. I built her palace in a night, with the help of Faërie. I raised me a Bridal Church, with the help of Faërie. But it could not be hallowed by Faërie. Prithee, who hallows my Church? I am waiting for Marriage Bells." Hereof are old Betrothals and their Bridal Songs.

Prince Starbeam bowed his head in veneration. The Priest and Keeper of the Precincts extended his hands over him and gave in plenary form the Ritual Benediction of the Stars. The virtue which flowed from his fingers made a halo of light about them, and at the end of the high office that light received him into the invisible mystery from which he had come forth.

Baptism of Contemplation in Faërie

The light had not faded round him who knelt in worship, nor the ecstasy of his contemplation ended when the cardinal glory of morning began to pour into the Minster through the moving pageant of a window behind the Altar and over against the East. In the strange dyes and

Speech of Windows in Faërie

tinctures of that living glass Prince Starbeam beheld a coronation which was not of Faërie, nor yet of the Golden Isles. He arose in fine, giving thanks to the Twelve Houses of Heaven, and then went out of the Minster walking backward, for he knew that the place was holy and a way of the Promise of Quest.

The Lord Royal received the report of his vision with little joy of heart, for he was in no wise reconciled to waiting, nor to the Quest of a Beloved Kinsman. He rebelled also from the notion of visions seen in his Palace or in his own Minster and he denied all share. Moreover, the Princess Cynthia had kept the covenants of the time, so that of all which passed in council between her and Prince Starbeam he learned nothing. But he saw by the light in her face that she had entered into peace and light. In fine, Prince Melnor beheld the Ring upon his deliverer, whereby he knew that he was preferred before himself by the Court of Stars at least, and his soul was drenched with bitterness.

World's End in Faërie: The End of Quest

The Quest of a Prince in Faërie

Prince Starbeam asked leave to depart, for the zeal of his Quest was upon him. His horse was brought round to the portal in chief of the Palace, against the mounting-post. The Lord Royal required him to leave the Ring as a gage of his quick return, and threatened disbelief of his vision, as one who had forgotten already the events which preceded his entrance. Prince Starbeam answered only that it was part of his quest to come and not even at a King's bidding could he surrender what he had received from the Court of Stars. Afterwards he assured the Lord Royal that great as was his kingly desire to confer upon one unworthy the favours belonging to the Ring, it could bear no comparison with his own longing to receive. "The desire of my Elect Lady is in the height and deep of my being. Rest certain that I shall not tarry. I will take unto me Wings of Quest, and I will take the Wings of

Faërie. I will come back to that which is mine, and I pray that the Houses of Heaven, in the majesty of their will and purpose, may vouchsafe to shorten the paths between."

"Choose therefore another horse," said the Lord Royal, "and it shall be the fleetest in all my stables; for he who proceeds on the business of this High Palace shall go well mounted, the better to attain his term and fulfil the royal pleasure."

Such an exchange was made accordingly, and whether or not the Lord Royal smothered his secret intent or had not as yet matured it, he said in parting: "Health and prosperity, Prince Starbeam: I greet the King in his coming."

Prince Starbeam answered: "To thee, my Lord Royal, the crown of all thy hopes, and a Queen on the Throne of Faërie."

The light of the morning received him into its heart of splendour, as he rode away in the morning, with his face to the East.

All the four-footed creatures and all the flying birds, and all the rushing fishes bring tidings of the Quest

XVII

BEGINNING OF TRAVELS IN FAËRIE

There are those who have come out upon a quiet shore and have stood by an everlasting sea: there are those who have heard the voices of the hills and the voice of green forests in Faërie. You can ask them over and over: there is always a cloud of witnesses. There are those also who know the Law of Quest and the way to the end therein. It is a law of single purpose, and Prince Starbeam carried it in his heart. But at this beginning of travel he carried also a deep searching of the King's purpose. Otherwise he might have returned to the old House in the waste and marish chase, thence only to make a start. As it was, he rode hard in the morning and onward still under the light of noon. He crossed a wide extent of forest-land, and then at the parting of roads he struck suddenly northwards, and left all beaten tracks presently in a world of hills. He was conscious within him of grace from the Magic Ring, even in the fibres of being. It is of faith that the horse felt it and answered the will of his master with love and understanding.

Of Losing and Finding in Faërie

Beasts on the side of goodness: such are the beasts of Faërie. Speak to us in your own tongue, all ye of field and fell. And you, O heart of love, shall give the key of meaning. The horse does not speak with the tongue of man, in Faërie or otherwhere; but the soul of a noble steed can commune with the soul of his master, if his are Faërie gifts. It came about therefore that the horse and his rider began to discourse together. "Whether to keep or to leave my valiant steed," so dreamed the soul of Prince

Starbeam. " I know not what dangers await me or how I shall be called to travel."

Language of the Heart in Faërie

The horse heard and answered after the same manner. " They will track you, my Prince and Master, because I am from the King's stables. I know my way and can find it. You shall presently send me back. I shall have served your purpose then. You are hard on the threshold of all the perils of Quest, and they are followed after another manner."

" Instruct me therefore, my prince of steeds at the manger."

" You will be hunted hither and thither, because the Lord Royal is set on seizing the Ring and finding some youth who is innocent respecting a Queen of Roses. He will not bide the time of the Perfect Quest. But you shall be helped and led, and will meet with another, to whom you will give the Magic Ring. It is not long thereafter to the finding of the Beloved Kinsman : it is not long to the Kinghood."

" Who has made thee so wise, my beautiful ? " Prince Starbeam asked, fondling his ropes of mane.

" That which I receive from those who watch in the hiddenness is that which I deliver to one who has ears within."

Counsels of Friendship in Faërie

Down the valley and over the lea, where the missel-thrush sang in the tawny light of that berry-brown afternoon : but again the road divided. O the meetings and partings in Faërie. The soul of the horse said to the soul of Prince Starbeam : " Here is the hour and the place." So the High Prince descended. He took the head of his bearer into the arms of love and kissed the star on his forehead between the speaking eyes. The steed whinnied, and the soul of the steed blessed him, with the formula of Faërie : " To you, my Prince in Kinghood." He went back by another way to the King's Palace. Very surely the beasts are human and the only brutes are monsters—

dragons and chimeras. The good living things in Faërie are raised to a higher stature.

Prince Starbeam followed his own path at random—understood as the path that he had chosen, for so far he had no certain guidance, except in the heart. The day drew towards evening; the Evening Star came out; the Star and the Magic Ring looked on the light of each other: perhaps it was only in fancy, perhaps in the truth of Faërie, that the bright jewel gave forth one note of sweetness under that liquid eye; but so it seemed to Prince Starbeam. Presently there were other luminaries, a great pageant in heaven. Yet shreds of the sunset still lighted his way where a village opened below him. He took the Magic Ring from his finger, and it was hidden safely in his breast.

Of Hiding and Finding in Faërie

This counsel of prudence followed, he went down a steep hill which led to the village, but came to a pause in the middle way of descent when he saw the brilliant uniform of one of the royal heralds in the little market-place. There were yokels and children about him, as he read in a loud voice from a scroll in his hands. Assured that this proclamation referred to himself, Prince Starbeam drew aside quickly into a shadow of fir-trees, awaiting whatever might follow. It befell, however, that the messenger mounted his horse and rode presently away, having affixed his notice to a post in the market-place. In a little while the villagers had scattered, the night fell, but there were lights in the cottage windows. So taking his chance in his hands, Prince Starbeam descended warily and could see at the head of the placard his own name in great letters, a faithful discovery of his appearance and of the horse on which he was mounted. He was accused of stealing a Magic Ring from the royal treasury: to whomsoever secured him a high prize was promised and death was threatened on all who harboured his person or abetted him in escape.

Wisdom is art in Faërie, and Prince Starbeam made himself as a silent ghost in the darkness: so for that time the night received him under sheltering wings. But for many days thereafter his ways of quest were rendered hard and perilous by unremitting pursuit. Wherever he went the Lord Royal's heralds had gone before already, and even in the humblest hamlets was the proclamation posted. There are those who are led unseen, as if by invisible friends, and there is above all the guiding spirit of Faërie, which is neither seen nor heard. But it shapes the ends decreed through paths of toil, because crowns are not had for the asking and places of peace are won.

It is told not what apples of the Kingdom, what fruit of life sustained him throughout those days of stress, for the tale of their episodes is only given in part, because of the great events which followed and their speaking pageants. It is told not what coverts received him for rest and sleep at need, or in what manner of raiment he sought to baffle the quest. But he came on a time of sunset to a lonely farm, far amidst folds of Faërie, and there he was taken in. Whence he came and whither he went they asked in words of welcome because of his toil-worn mien; and if Prince Starbeam answered in simple words, yet were they words of parable, though a heart of truth was in them. But they sat down to meat in the supper-room, and amidst its old-world plenty the farmer's daughter, a very fair maiden, setting more food on his plate, asked archly in a whisper: "Where then is the Magic Ring?"

Opening of Doors in Faërie

So was his secret uncovered and he was known through all his veils. His only hope threw him on the faith of his host, who said that he was surely with friends and asked to see the Ring. But Prince Starbeam explained that it was now in a place of the hiddenness, and in the strain of a silence which followed, from under long eyelashes, the maiden in heart's desire looked at the beautiful youth, while the clock chimed in the kitchen.

The supper was over but flagons were still on the table and the farmer alone with his guest, whom he offered his daughter to wife if the guest gave her the Ring.

The Air gives up Brides in Faërie

" The day of my marriage is far as yet," said Prince Starbeam, " and I am called meanwhile into another country."

" It is a woman's dowry," said the farmer in a vexed tone, " and I will do anything to secure it to my daughter."

" The Magic Ring is a Gift of the Court of Stars," Prince Starbeam answered, " and I am its warden only at this time. A pure maiden may well be meant to receive it, and if it be their will it shall be delivered without price."

The farmer thought now that his guest was surely mad; but he affirmed only: " My daughter is a pure virgin, and she will thank you for the gift of the Ring."

Prince Starbeam said: " I will call on the Evening Star."

" Heaven bless you: sleep here," the farmer answered, and he led him upstairs to a room where there was a bed hung with curtains of white linen, embroidered with the sign of the House, an inverted triangle of three Ravens swooping. The farmer would have helped him to undress, hoping that somehow he might see the Magic Ring; but Prince Starbeam knelt down, as if for the promised invocation, and so was he left by his host. He prayed, however, for the general guidance and purification of his heart in life, that he might know the will of the Stars, and when he had finished, his resolution was to watch for one hour and endeavour thereafter to leave the house secretly. About midway in the vigil the door of his room opened softly, and moonlight fell on the face of the farmer's youngest son. In his eyes was peace of vision, and there on the threshold he made the sign of silence, closing the door behind him and advancing with still steps.

"You are in sore peril," he whispered; "I am here to warn and help. They will take the Ring of your Enchantment. Follow me therefore, because there is one way by which you can make an escape. When you have found it, let me see your Sacred Ring, and I will shew you my Seering Glass, which is full of visions."

"What do you see in your crystal?" Prince Starbeam asked.

"I see all the Houses of Faërie, the Land of Stars and Land of the Bright Spirits. It has told me your name," added the farmer's son. "You are Prince Starbeam."

The Eye and the Vision in Faërie

The boy took him by the hand and led him through narrow passages to a bare room, the window of which he opened, making no sound, and pointed to the thatched and sloping roof of a shed beneath. Setting the example to Prince Starbeam, he crept out and sliding down the inclined plane on to which he had stepped, he dropped quietly on the earth at a few feet below the projecting eaves. Prince Starbeam followed, and then—taking his hand again—the boy led him, under the shadow of stables, through straggling yards. A wicket-gate beyond opened on moonlit meadows, which they crossed in breathless haste and so emerged through a hedge into a green lane, shadowed by tall elms and hawthorns. The path descended steeply, and the lane brought them at length into a broad white road.

"Here is the Magic Ring," said Prince Starbeam, as they paused before parting, and he dropped it for a few moments into the boy's sun-browned palm. The lad's eyes glistened, as he balanced it against a small globe which shone in the moonlight, a heavy crystal, in the hollow of his other hand.

"Let us call on the Court of Stars," said Prince Starbeam.

"Perchance it has willed that you shall be the next Keeper of the Ring, and I may be only its warden."

But the boy shook his head. "The Angel of the crystal has promised to take me into his Land of Vision, and I want not the Magic Ring or to live for ever on earth: it is brighter in the World of Vision."

"Let me see your visions," said Prince Starbeam.

They sat side by side in a sheltered nook and gazed in the seering-glass. In a few moments both saw, each after his own manner, in the pellucid deeps. That which was shewn to Prince Starbeam was the Daughter of the Stars standing in the wild garden of her Holy Lodge, watching the phantom characters of the Star-Language as they passed across the ebony disc of her wondrous instrument. But the farmer's son beheld the transfigured apparition of Prince Starbeam as he came out of Faërie, bathed in the smile of the Queen-Regent and crowned with her star-kiss. Prince Starbeam called the image of the Beloved Kinsman into the seering-glass and he failing appealed to the gift of vision in the farmer's son. When this proved vain also —as if prompted by a sudden impulse—he held the Magic Ring over the crystal, so that a ray of its light fell on the lucent sphere. A cloud formed therein and then, parting suddenly, discovered letters as if written by the ray in characters of light, but they were in the Secret Language of the Stars.

A Glass of Vision in Faërie

"What does that mean?" asked the farmer's son, breathless.

"I shall know when I am King," his companion answered sadly, as he prepared to depart.

Seek and Find is written in the Glass of Vision

The boy looked at him, with soft eyes full of worship. They passed to the middle of the road and stood with the moonlight on them. Prince Starbeam took his preserver in his arms and, as a Son of Destiny, invoked on him the blessing of the Everlasting Stars: he wished him joy in the Land of Vision, the love of angels and lucidity of soul for ever. In the GREAT REGISTER OF FAËRIE and in the RECORDS OF THE COURT OF STARS it is testified that the farmer's son went up the Golden Stairs and that he saw the Marriage of the King.

Twelve manners of moon in Faërie, but who knows which of them set as Prince Starbeam pursued his course? The morning came thereafter and voices of spirits at morning because of the Magic Ring. But yesterday, to-day and—as it seemed—for ever the chase went on. I have heard that he hid among bracken while horses and riders passed; I have heard that he crossed the water; there are rumours of wreck and of rescue, whether on lake or sea. I have heard of wooded valleys, and he tarried in valleys of silence, where the silence held his name on a threshold of speaking. There are houses in lonely woods and grey towers by very secret meres which keep the memory of his presence. There is also a wind of the spirit breathing through haunted chambers or softly in echoing halls, and the uttered name is his. But the next story which adds a link to the chain says that a certain chase was continued from village to village, and Prince Starbeam flying before it came to the bleak shore of the lonely ocean, when heavy clouds covered the face of heaven. The receding tide took out the grey cold sea, a penetrating mist began to fall, and he sought shelter in one of the many caves which honey-combed frowning cliffs. At a certain bend thereof, far out of sight alike from shore and main, he piled up dry drift-wood and kindled a fire to warm him.

Beyond the Land of Clouds is a Land of Light

An hour of darkness was upon him. He had taken unto him wings of quest and in the thinking heart he had taken fleet wings of Faërie, but the term towards which he strove was shrouded more deeply than heaven was veiled above in that place and its hour. But all who have passed through the waste places and dwelt in deserted cities know well that the sown and green are found on a further side, as well as the haunts of men, and that after dark in the night-tide there is joy poured out in the morning on the other side of the gate which leads everywhere. It came about therefore that Prince Starbeam drew forth from the cavern to find that the sky had cleared and that over the turbid sea shone the great Court of Stars. As he contemplated, with the wind around him beating invisible wings, out of the shadow of rocks emerged the figure of a youth, approaching and calling. The heart of Prince Starbeam, startled, leaped for a moment only as he thought of his hunted days; but of music and not of menace was the voice he heard, while the rising moon revealed the face of the youth and his fair eyes, as a light of heaven for clearness. He was clad richly, though soiled from head to foot with the dust of long travelling, and he asked whether there was a village along the coast with a chance of shelter. When he heard that the place was wild and far from human haunts, he sighed as one who is weary, at which Prince Starbeam added: "There is a cavern in this cliff which is warm and dry, and I look to sleep for the night on its weeds and moss: if you will, it is yours to share," and he led the way.

Lights that lead in Faërie

The fire was burning clearly and there was little smoke. He who was Master of the House heaped dry seaweed before it and took the shoes from the swollen feet of his guest. He had food also in a wallet and a flask of spring water. Refreshed after this manner, they gave their names to each other, Prince Starbeam pledging his companion and he crying out in his gladness: "I have found thee at last, my Prince." And so laying his head on the breast of him whom he had sought, presently he fell asleep. It might be an hour or more that Prince Starbeam sat supporting him, weaving his chain of dream while the fire sparkled and glowed. Then he laid the lad to rest, pillowed on weeds, and was soon in sleep beside him.

There are voices which go through enchantment and awaken sleepers therein. There is sleep which opens into a world of vision. Was it in such an awakening that Prince Starbeam was aware suddenly of a great light about him, an embodied face of vision, uplifting of hands in Faërie and healing light of hands? The speech of the old ocean echoed without the cave, like speech of the waters of Faërie, and all that it tells to those who stand by the shore and listen became alive in his heart. It was stilled also within, as music stays the winds, when the voice of that vision which came from the Court of Stars delivered their new message. It was like another link in a chain, a stage in the quest which he followed to find the Beloved Kinsman, the world to come in Faërie and the crown therein. The voice and the message ordained the Magic Ring to another Keeper, and this was Prince Eulis.

The World beyond all Seeing

O words caught and missed, secret voices of all: O high seas sounding on the sands without. There was light no more in the cavern; the vision withdrawn therefrom left dark of dark. It was after a space only that Prince Starbeam saw in the dull glow of the embers his companion seated erect and a glory of great wonder shining through lambent eyes.

"I have heard all," said Prince Eulis: "I saw the Messenger of Heaven, as I wakened from dreams beside you, and I know what he said. I am sent to you by a Star-Spirit."

They piled up drift-wood on the fire and held their vigil beside it.

"Tell me your story," said Prince Starbeam, as he held up the boy's hand and ringed it then and there.

Prince Eulis kissed him on the forehead, the eyes and mouth in a passion of sacred worship and told his tale in the flickering lights and shadows, while the smoke curled upwards and was buffeted from point to point on the jagged roof. The voice of the speaker mingled with hollow murmurs of the sea, and Prince Starbeam beheld more often the moving pictures rather than heard with ears the words of their sequence. The dawn came up as it ended, and they went out of the cavern. The shadows of light were passing, an endless rout, over the crested waves: the dews in the path of the sun freshened the way of morning, and the red gold eastward blazed upon the open main. The mystery-words of the sea and roll of its far-off voices came to shore with the tide. There is new thought in the morning, the light makes all things new. In its radiant pageant Prince Starbeam beheld the end and crown of quest: it seemed not far to the Kinghood, however the years rolled on.

Speech of Waters in Faërie

"Tell me your own story," Prince Eulis prayed, as they sat on a rock together in the morning glory, looking seaward. When this also was ended they locked their hands and lips, like those who part for ever after an hour of service. And one from another henceforward they followed divided ways.

Who rides on a white horse through places of silence? Son of the Court of Stars, they have mounted you well and nobly: we know not whom. . . . Over the meadows about the precincts of Faërie, over the fragrant byways, carpets of flowers here on the hither side, who fares through the Golden Isles? . . . Does a Lord Royal await you, Child of the Ring?

The heart of the hill in Faërie and the high heart of the sea

XVIII

THE QUEST OF A SOUL IN FAËRIE

In a land that is very far away, yet nearer than flower and leaf on a bush of roses, Prince Eulis—because of his beauty—was called Faërie Prince. His father was one of those Kings who had followed the flight of strange ways which encompass Faërie, and he had found the Stone of Wealth. They dwelt in a marble Palace, encompassed by a glittering court: without doubt the most fortunate of princes was Eulis. For him chiefly the sun might be said to shine; for him the birds sang through the live-long day; rare flowers exhaled their fragrance; and ever the winds breathed softly round the palace of Prince Eulis and about his favourite pavilion. It has been said that his father was a King, but all who dwelt in the Palace were peers of high estate, kinsmen or sons of Kings. The resources of the world about them were taxed for their delight, the ways of plenty in Faërie and the ways of feasting. The cornflowers in fields opened blue deeps like ocean; the sunflowers in gardens shone with a solar glory; there was a moon as of heaven in the moonwort; the bluebells rang chimes together; the starwort had stolen Orion. Oblations of bread on a platter were as the food of Eden and a star was in every cup. The pipes of the pipers were answered all over the forest and fell, till all life span to music.

The False Faërie is Seeming

One day a stranger presented himself at the gates: he was tall and lean, his garments were of uncouth fashion and coarse material; his face was dark, pallid and very earnest; his dusk eyes had a light in them which radiated

Of Strangers cast by Tempest on Shores of Faërie

with inward fire. He represented himself as a shipwrecked traveller and asked permission to display before the company, which assembled each evening in the Palace, some mirrors with peculiar properties, since they could not fail to entertain the King and his guests.

There was something in the speaker's voice and mien that awed those whom he addressed, and when the stranger had retired, with his prayer granted, they remained subdued and thoughtful. The haunting voice had stirred deep wells of memory: for one it seemed the tones of his mother calling him in childhood from glens and woodlands to his home; another remembered the deep murmur of the sea, as he had heard it in youth and had longed for the free life of a rover; while in the ears of a third rang faintly and far away a convent bell, and he remembered how once he had served at a high altar. Thus each was carried to a sacred moment of life or the memory of a great intention.

Soon after sunset the stranger presented himself again at the Palace and was admitted to a hall where the company had already gathered. Here his lean figure, outlandish garb and awkward air caused a certain diversion; but his quiet manner did not alter: only a glinting light in his eyes shewed that the raillery had not passed unnoticed. He uncovered his mirrors, which had been concealed under his cloak, and after wiping the surfaces he set one of them in an upright position on a table, where the clear glass contrasted curiously with the tarnished frame.

Speaking now for the first time, he proceeded thus in a kind of monotonous chant: "By the faculty of ordinary sight we become acquainted with the surface of things, and one aspect of their being is presented thus; but it hides rather than reveals their real nature. Let us imagine superadded to this normal gift a higher mode of vision, by which minds would perceive the essence, not the appearance of objects: then would a new heaven be revealed and a new earth, with the radiant dwellers therein. But for its full and free exercise the soul must be dwelling at its highest, and hence the gift is at best occasional only for most people in the world. By the knowledge which I have gained in my travels I have sought to make others see some part at least of the hidden side of things, as it were, in a kind of vision. This mirror has certain properties which are like fire and light in the heart, or zeal of quest in Faërie."

The other Side of a Glass

All crowded forward eagerly and beheld in the mirror on the table a mellow twilight deepening in heaven. They stood, as if in a garden, looking eastward over green bushes, where a solitary twig was lifted above its peers towards the violet sky and a single bright star. Was it possible that this was all, and who indeed had not seen it? With unbelieving hearts and mockingly, they turned towards the stranger, who read their thoughts and answered: "A certain harmony between the mind and Nature is required to open reality. It is like a stillness of spiritual dream, stillness intent with life, a settlement of all things small and mean as a sediment, leaving the clear air of living intelligence for the medium through which all is seen. In such a mood I have stood myself by the spot which is offered here to your notice, and I know that a Land of Soul's Desire extends beyond it."

The Moon rises in Faërie

This explanation sounded past comprehension, so its hearers turned to the mirror and gazed again therein. The night had deepened there, the orange tint had faded from the sky, the star had risen and brightened, but it revealed rather than dissolved the lucent darkness about it. And now there was a movement in the bushes, as if a gentle wind had passed over them, while the sky began to fill with light. The spectators bent forward eagerly, expecting a marvel. The light expanded and heightened, till there came into view the fragment of a disc shining on the landscape's verge, and at length a full moon of great brilliance and beauty flooded earth and heaven with its beams. The spectators rebelled in their anger, crying out: "What is this you tell us? Have we not known from our childhood how a moon rises in the East?"

"Without doubt," the stranger answered, undisturbed, "and if your lives are prolonged, you will know it again and again. But had you beheld it with eyes of soul rather than body of flesh, repetition would seem never too frequent. Here is a threshold of reality, but it is your misfortune to have lost your souls, or otherwise they are asleep within you. For a moment, however, I can supply some part of what is wanting."

He passed his right hand several times over the glass, while a thin flame seemed to follow its motion and hover for a few moments over the surface of the mirror. It faded, and he bade them look once more. The Kaleidoscope Kingdom of this world had turned in the glass of Faërie and become another world of wonder. The moon was still shining, but like a dream which is seen in a dream, with rays diffused over the whole atmosphere and brooding nimbus-like above the green bushes. Even as they gazed it seemed that the light increased till the lunar disc was hidden. There were purple paths in the mid-light, ways of violet, expanses of orange beyond them. These in fine dissolved and gave back the orbed moon, which opened doors like those of a great temple, and a throng poured forth, as of Heralds and Keepers of Mysteries, or of souls which go forward in vision. To those who looked, it seemed for a few moments as a sudden opening of windows at the four quarters of Faërie, giving on a new world. To one it was a following of streams and coming forth upon great waters; for another the contemplation of secrets held in deep brown wells; a third, as with his ear to earth, caught whispers of the under-world. And still the throng

Wealth of the World Wonderful

poured forth, a host of presences filling the world with meanings and even the vacant heart. But a moment came when those who felt and saw broke out in words of wonder, at which a cloud formed on the mirror and the scene ended. They begged to look once more, but the stranger shook his head, saying: "You have destroyed it by your own acts and now it cannot be recovered. There is, however, another picture in the mirror, and this I can shew you."

He wiped the surface with the cloth in which the glass had been wrapped and then invited their attention. A little lake lay in the bosom of an embowering wood—a sunny lake, reflecting a blue sky. Some water-lilies floated at one end and on the further side a party of village boys bathed in the clear water, while others were stretched on the bank and through leaves overhead the sunbeams glistened on their white flesh, dappling it with light and shadow.

The Bank of Wild Thyme is ever a Place of Vision

"A fair picture," said the stranger, "but you have seen it surely, and often."

"Yes," answered one of the company, and yet with hesitation in his voice, while the rest were silent.

The figure of a tall man entered now upon the left, as if to watch the happy group of lads before him, and at once the scene transfigured. Light and shade and colour were blended according to another law than that of normal Nature, and thus the world opened a deeper heart of its wonder. Nature is like an outer garment and Faërie is like a garment within; but after these there is the inward loveliness, without vesture or veil. It seemed for a moment that those who looked in the mirror beheld this mystery of being, though they knew not what they saw. They saw in truth another side of humanity and the grace thereof. Their breath came hard and fast in their great rapture and longing; but when the figure in the glass turned his face and they saw that it was the stranger himself, a cry of astonishment went forth, while a black curtain of night fell upon the scene.

"Your reward is with you," said the stranger in a severe voice. "But once more and once only you shall look upon this glass of vision. Keep therefore its law of silence, lest worse befall," and he obliterated with his cloth the last remnants of the former scene.

The picture now presented was simpler still: it was a woodland glen, through an opening in which the sky shone bright and cloudless.

"Rest and simplicity," said the stranger in a voice that thrilled his hearers, "are like magic mirrors which reveal the inward sense behind the outward signs. Stars also speak and planets move in music."

Light in the Place of Light

As before, he passed his hand over the mirror, and where alone the blue sky had been visible shone now the radiant face of a spirit, and above it a star of the first magnitude. The eyes were raised towards it in a calm of sacred contemplation. O life-giving eyes of beauty, they were turned presently and looked on those who beheld them, their light embosoming light, glory of pure intelligence, as a world of mind unveiled. The spirit raised its hands, and from the five fingers of each there streamed a golden radiance, which passed through the glass of vision and fell on the faces of the spectators. They started back dazzled, with cries of fear, and the mirror, with a loud crash, splintered into a thousand pieces.

Tears stood in the eyes of the stranger. "There is no soul here," he said. "No light from within leaped up to meet that light, which was blinding to the eyes of sense alone." And so sorrowing, he gathered the shards of his glass into the cloth which had held it.

The silence of a great fear fell upon the whole company; but in the end they began to excuse themselves and offer compensation to the stranger for his grievous loss. " Your loss is greater than mine," he answered quietly.

Prince Eulis had watched with delight the pictures shewn in the mirror and had listened full of wonder to the explanations given by its owner. " Will you take me to those radiant scenes ? " he asked the stranger, with clasped hands. " Where shall I seek them ? " He had no answer in words, but the stranger smiled upon him and looked stedfastly into the beautiful eyes of the boy. It was as if the heart of Prince Eulis said to him : " The time is not yet : but there is to-day and to-morrow in Faërie : wait for the day of vision."

The second mirror was placed upright on the table.

The Mirror speaks in Faërie

" Your eyes could not bear that light which fell on them from the hands of benediction uplifted by the Star-Spirit," said the stranger after a pause, " and the reason is that unhappily you are without souls, as I fear may be presently revealed to you. Here is a Magic Mirror which reflects the soul instead of the body of man. It appears as a sacred flame which is sometimes one of great light. I have seen it wax and wane ; I have seen it quenched for a time : I have seen it in glory of glory. Some persons looking herein reflect neither flame nor light : these are without souls. I ask you to look in this glass and tell me that which you see."

Some pressed forward, feeling quite certain that they possessed a soul, and these retired disappointed. Others declined altogether to consult the mirror, saying that they had no wish to suffer humiliation from the stranger, who was evidently a man of ill-will ; while the rest looked languidly and were neither surprised nor dejected when the glass gave back no light.

" We have felt no need of this soul about which you speak," they said, " and beyond doubt it is of little use or value."

"Good sir," asked one, "perhaps it might be possible to purchase a soul, since most things can be bought with money. But would any profit arise from such a possession?"

Prince Eulis was among those who came forward eagerly to consult the mirror, and tears started in his eyes when he fared no better than the rest. He longed to question the stranger, but there was a babel of voices round him, voices of those who jested, those who aired a grievance and those who produced their purses, demanding the price of a soul. The mysterious visitor waved the clamourers aside and retired with no further words; but the boy's tears did not fall unheeded by one who possessed that seeing sense which divines the final end and knows that it must come to pass.

Beginnings of Quest in Faërie

Much as they had been astonished and even awed at heart, the impression on most of the spectators wore quickly away, leaving only resentment against him who had made them conscious of their own deficiencies. It was otherwise with Prince Eulis, to whom the stranger's visit was like an epoch in life and over whose spirit there came the kind of change which marks the passing of joy. Many times over he asked his parents and others concerning the soul and its nature; but they knew and cared nothing, while the stranger was cursed earnestly for distressing an innocent boy.

One of the secrets in Faërie is to wish well, and it came about later that Prince Eulis in the midst of his longing received the help of a dream. The stranger stood beside him, radiant in the likeness of that Star-Spirit who appeared in the Magic Mirror. "Prince Eulis," he said at length, "thou shalt find thy soul."

"Tell me when, tell me where," entreated the eager boy. The spirit smiled and vanished, lifting up his arms of light, and in the music which followed the boy heard in the darkness a counsel of dream: "Prince Starbeam; seek out Prince Starbeam."

The Quest of Light in Faërie

The next morning his bed was empty: he had departed in the night. The palace-dwellers had no task in divining the cause of his absence: he had gone to seek his soul. They fell down on their knees and invoked the judgment of the Everlasting Stars on the head of that infamous stranger who had wiled the hapless Prince into such unprofitable courses. This done, they returned to their pleasures, and the existence of Prince Eulis was almost forgotten, and that at no distant date, even by his parents, who were consoled for his loss by the birth of other children.

All things lead on the quest, but that which they lead is the heart of the earnest seeker, turned to the heart of Faërie. Prince Eulis travelled eastward—as it seemed to him, for days without number. Be it marked, the old chronicle says, that no one shall fail of his quest, be it ever so hard or high, if he fare towards the rising or setting sun, and he shall meet with great adventures. In a certain hour of noon Prince Eulis ascended a lofty hill and came at its further side to a forest of fir-trees, which lay on the left of the road, while a little gate on the right gave entrance to a meadow on the southern slope of the hill. Far away was a city of the sea, the blue waters of which looked dim in their mist of light. The deep valley below sheltered a village gathered about an old church. Around and beyond spread hills and forests, white roads winding between hedges and narrow footpaths over open fields. Shrill voices of children were borne on the fragrant air, and the church-bells were ringing.

Paths of Mercy and Judgment

Prince Eulis went down to the village, where a man of crazed aspect stood by the burn-side, exhibiting the picture of a beautiful lady to the crowd of yokels. This was the artist who once on a time had painted the Princess Cynthia.

Thereafter he sought in vain for a Magic Ring and becoming distracted went wandering over the world, shewing the portrait of his idol and recording his own misfortunes. Prince Eulis listened to his story till the painter went his way. The boy also walked towards the distant city, dreaming on what he had heard.

"If ever I find my soul," he thought, "I will go in search of the Magic Ring."

A village priest passed on the road, for there was service to be held in the church.

"Father," the boy asked, "I pray you, what is the soul?"

Lore of Souls

"My son," answered the priest, "the soul has been defined by theologians as a simple and indivisible substance which the Great Star-Master breathes into man and which henceforth will subsist for ever."

"Thou art wise indeed," said the youth, "but where shall I find Prince Starbeam?"

"There is no such prince in this royalty."

"In that case, I must go further."

"The stars follow you," said the priest, as they parted: but for long after the boy wondered and repented that he had asked nothing concerning the Star-Master who gives the soul to men.

After long travellings Prince Eulis met Prince Starbeam and received from him the Magic Ring, which he bore to the Golden Isles. It was now middle summer, some two years after he left his father's palace in a time of the blossoming of almonds. The report of his coming spread through the country-side and reached the royal court, where years and their passing had brought about great changes. After the departure of Prince Starbeam the heralds of the Lord Royal had sought him over the whole kingdom. Proclamations were made and great rewards offered; ambassadors were sent to neighbouring kingdoms with fair words of petition and to distant tributary principalities with long orders. Prince Starbeam was outlawed and the High Star-Priest was induced by the kind of persuasions which cover up kingly threats to excommunicate the vanished youth and pronounce a curse upon him, according to ancient form.

These precautions notwithstanding, the Lord Royal lived to experience the failure of all his plans. Affliction was followed by sickness, and when death drew to the threshold he summoned his Lords in Council, whom he pledged to continue the quest of the Magic Ring and accept as their King whomsoever might possess the treasure. He called also his daughter and would have sworn her in like manner to wed him who should come with the proper warrants; but the ministering angel set on him a seal of silence.

When the time of mourning was ended, the Princess Cynthia was crowned Queen of the Golden Isles, awaiting the King to come. Her first act invited the High Star-Priest to rescind the sentence pronounced against Prince Starbeam; the next restored his rights and he was declared free to revisit his native land whenever he so desired. For twelve months and over she reigned a star of peace, and already the common people worshipped her goodness, when rumours reached the palace that a Prince with a Magic Ring had crossed the sea and was coming to claim the daughter of the Lord Royal. It was ascertained that his name was Eulis, a tall and comely youth with the blue of heaven in his eyes. He was said further to be alone and worn with travel, and deeply were the maids of the country in love with the gallant lad.

Meridian Days in Faërie

The Queen heard this in silence and withdrew sorrowing. If her heart in the earlier days had been given to Prince Melnor, the soul of Prince Starbeam had drawn her soul to him, and it is known that in such cases the heart of flesh follows. So she thought deeply within her: "If this

Prince Eulis should come indeed to love me, there will be dole for both, and little good will follow."

Standing in the recess of a great window as the violet twilight fell, she said also, but later: "I am a coward to seek flight, yet with great fear do I fear this new heartache. Let Prince Eulis reign over the Golden Isles if my father has willed it, but over me he can never reign. O Sacred Court of Stars, give unto me grace of deliverance. And thou, Evening Star, trembling in heaven above me, if it may be that thou wilt do so, take thy Ring."

With dim eyes she sat down trembling in an old high-backed chair by the oriel. Her white hands fell listlessly on her lap, and the Magic Ring gleamed strangely in the darkness. The night deepened and a white mist rolled up from far-away marshes. Palaces of Faërie, gramarye of endless rooms, is there rest for the heart of the weary, anywhere, anywhere within your world of walls?

Grace of Leading in Faërie

About twelve the door of the chamber was thrown open. The Queen rose, and a youth of fair aspect entered habited in white samite and bearing a wand of peace. He called on the Queen to follow him and taking her hand in his, they went out in silence. As they passed over the threshold, Cynthia whispered in her heart: "This is a Messenger from the Evening Star."

They descended a marble staircase, and her hand quivered on the balustrade. In the great hall below it was her own heart which said to her: "Surely this is the Beloved Kinsman, who is called the Brother of Prince Starbeam."

They went into the open air and paused in a portico of the palace. The cold mist curdled the blood in the veins of the Queen; but looking forth with her bright, gentle, human eyes, she said almost audibly: "Without doubt, this night I shall pass to the Court of Stars." And touching a golden gong, she summoned her maidens, and bade seven of them follow her.

The lips of the youth were lighted with a faint smile, and descending twelve steps the whole train passed through the palace grounds to the bank of a broad river. There are ships that pass in the darkness and ships in the moonlight pass, over the waters of Faërie. They entered a great barge which was moored near at hand; the youth, standing in the stern, took the rudder; and with the tide, the wind and the mist, they moved onward.

The Search for an Asylum in Faërie

" We are going on a strange journey," said the Queen. And the maidens wondered, and there was a long silence. Which of them knew that the greatest voyage of all is from West to East in Faërie?

" We are going into a far country," the Queen said. Her maidens wondered and sighed, and there was a long silence.

" Very surely we are going to the Court of Stars," said the Queen. And the maidens wondered and wept, for all had lovers at home, and there was a long, long silence.

The seven maidens drew close together, with their arms about each other, pale and cold and frightened. They heard weeping within the mountains, sounds of tears falling in still places: who bruised the heart of Faërie? The beautiful eyes of the youth were fixed far in front, piercing the white mist. The deep rapid river drew them onward; vast trees, seen dimly on either bank, rustled their leaves and clashed their branches mournfully in the night wind; the heart of the Queen was hushed within her; and no one spoke in the barge: it was sad, long silence.

At last the mist lifted, the moon shone through, the waters gleamed beneath, the vault of heaven was high and clear above them: there were stars without number, and the sea shone in front. As they drew to the river's mouth, they discovered, ascending from the left bank—which was sand of the sea—a Golden Staircase going up into heaven.

Moons f Quest

Its summit was lost in the blue altitude and in the moonlight sheen it reflected strange, quivering light.

"What is this Golden Staircase?" cried Cynthia to her Guide, as she rose erect in the barge. "Where will it lead us?"

"It will take thee, O Queen, into Starland, even the Court of Stars," the youth answered.

"The way is long to the end: my friends, will you follow me thither or, friends of mine, go back?"

"It is a dizzy journey," said the eldest. "Gracious Lady, when should we reach there? How should we return?"

The Queen in silence turned to the Guide, who stepped ashore, and with hand extended helped her to leave the barge. This done, and the prow being turned to the beach, he spurned it lightly with his left foot, saying: "The parting of waters in Faërie."

The barge veered round and moved slowly up stream. The maidens shrieked and held out arms towards their mistress, who, standing with clasped hands on the sea-shore, gazed after them weeping, and then followed her Guide, who began to ascend the staircase. At some distance up she paused, white and trembling, her tall fair body swayed by an inward dread and desolation. She leaned over and through pallid mists of night saw the barge moving slowly, propelled against wind and tide, the moonlight gleaming on the white garments and white scared faces of the maidens. The Guide tarried three steps above, his head turned away. The Magic Ring shone in the searching air as her hand rested on the crystal balustrade. At length she looked toward him, who pointed upward where the endless staircase wound. She drew a veil over her face and obeyed. At the third further step he took her hand, and so led—with face averted—in thought following the barge long after it was lost to sight and the view itself

Of those who come no more

had merged in the mist and moonbeams, the Royal Lady of the Golden Isles went up the Golden Staircase to the Court of Stars, for her dedication in the life of the Ring.

A few hours after midnight the barge grounded on a waste place of the river bank, it might be, a mile from the palace. The maidens landed, dew-drenched and terrified. The mist was still moving over low meadows and marshland; it was thick also on the river; and as they stepped on saturated grass, the barge began to drop once more silently down stream. It was full morning and over when they sank on the marble steps leading to the first court of the palace. Confusion reigned therein, for it had been known since daybreak that the Queen and her virgins had gone away. The wildest rumours were afloat; the Lords in Council met hastily, and mounted messengers were already scouring the country when the High Star Priest entered leading a youth, of whom it was observed immediately that he carried the missing Magic Ring, or an amazing counterpart.

The Bond and Faith of Rings

It was well known that Prince Eulis was on his way thither, but his green years disappointed the nobles, no less than his arrival in the care of the Star Priest, who represented a competitive power, at once disliked and feared. The Prince had been found wandering in the city on the previous night by the priest himself and he had prayed for shelter, reciting his name and purpose, and explaining that he could not present himself at the palace in his travel-worn guise. The virtues of the Magic Ring had been scouted from the beginning by the priestly caste in the city, and the old man contemplated the gem with a faint satirical smile. The Prince, however, was a precious acquisition, and he was welcomed readily in the Holy House, where the priests themselves served him and provided all things needful for his state and claims.

When he had been refreshed further by convent food, the High Star Priest signed to his inferior brethren and they left him alone with the youth. He, who had dreamed that his troubles were ended with the Quest itself was now to learn in disillusion that they had not as yet begun; that powerful nobles would resent the elevation of a wandering youth to universal dominion, whatever the guerdon borne, while the Queen herself would be persuaded hardly to accept a new lover, seeing that she mourned an old one. The help which the High Star Priest passed on to offer warily, in the name of the power behind him, seemed so needful that the terms mattered little, and Prince Eulis was pledged to his adviser, who sent him to his couch, happy in the assurance of his strong co-operation.

The Power of the Keys in Faërie

When the news of the Queen's disappearance reached the High Star Priest next morning he refused at first to credit so wild a story; but when it was confirmed abundantly he repaired to the palace with Prince Eulis. The return of the Queen's maidens occurred at the same time; they told their wonderful tale; and the High Priest, all his astuteness notwithstanding, was completely bewildered.

After long deliberation the State Council decided to await the Queen's return for a year and a day, before electing her successor. "The Kingdom is in the sacred care of the Stars," said the High Priest. But the Leaders in Council answered, "It shall be in the hands of the Commonweal," which meant their own hands. Thereon the High Priest took charge of Prince Eulis as Heir-Designate of Royalty by the will of the Court of Stars. Now, the priestly caste was a power in that realm; and it came to pass that it succeeded. When the appointed time had expired he was crowned in the Temple, and the State Council became a thing of no effect from that day.

Prince Eulis had grown into a stately and beautiful

youth; he kept his word faithfully to the priestly caste, and received at their hands the title of King Immortal. His legend says that he became great among kings and princes under his star of peace. The people prospered and were happy; new cities rose up and great temples were built therein. At sunrise each morning the King Immortal went up into a high tower and had great joy of his possessions, believing that they would be his for ever because of the Magic Ring. Yet he questioned sometimes within himself concerning the soul, and once on a day he asked the High Star Priest respecting its nature. When he heard again that it was the immortal principle conferred on man, he comforted himself and smiled, saying: "I have surely found my soul: my soul is in this Sacred Ring."

Sacraments of Names in Faërie

And so the days passed on, telling out years of life: the old High Priest died, and Prince Eulis stood now in the radiant zenith of manhood. One day a stranger presented himself at the gates. He was tall and lean; his garments were of uncouth fashion and coarse material; his face was pallid, dark and full of earnestness; there was a light in his eyes which seemed to radiate from the mind within. He represented himself as a traveller from the East and sought secret audience of the King Immortal.

"King Immortal," said the stranger, when the monarch deigned to receive him, "in my travels through the far countries I have met with hidden knowledge, and there is power of transmission to those who are proved worthy. There is in particular one division which is called Secret of Secrets and Key of Keys concerning a Golden Staircase, a way to the Court of Stars, and the leading of Magic Rings. Some part of my lesser secrets has been given to those who produced a test of merit, but this concerns thyself, and thee also must I prove, O King. Here is a Magic Mirror which reflects the soul instead of the body of man. It appears as a sacred flower which is sometimes one of great light. I have seen it wax and wane; I have seen it quenched for a time; I have seen it in glory of glory. Some persons who look herein reflect neither flower nor light: these are without souls, and not unto such shall be given the hidden knowledge which I have met with in far countries, but much less that which is Secret of Secrets and Key of Keys. Look therefore, O King, in this Mirror and tell me that which thou seest."

"Master," said the King Immortal, as, white to the lips, he came down from his high state, "well indeed do I know thee."

The stranger smiled and answered, pointing with his lean hand to the Mirror: "Know also thyself, O King."

O Glass of Truth

It seemed for a space no longer the great monarch but the fair boy Prince Eulis who gazed steadfastly in the magic disc and waited vainly, with a deepening sense of humiliation, for a light to kindle within it. But when he removed his eyes it was the King Immortal who said with defiant pride: "My soul is in the Ring that I wear: disease and age and death can never overtake me. What is this vaunted soul of which thou speakest but the principle of perpetual life? If therefore I be immortal, I have surely found my soul."

As he spoke, he held up the Magic Ring before the Magic Mirror. For a moment no image was reflected, and then the coil of a serpent devouring its own tail appeared in its clear depth, as if the circle of the Ring were magnified many times therein. With a cry like a boy's or a woman's, the King Immortal fell in a swoon on the floor. When he came at length to himself, to find that he was alone, he summoned pages and courtiers, telling them to recall the stranger. But messengers despatched in all directions failed to follow his track; the sentinels at the gates had not seen him, nor the patrols in the city without.

The King Immortal was silent and deep in thought on the day which followed thereafter, as one whose light has turned into great darkness and whose cup of life is poisoned. The Magic Ring shone on his hand as of old, but about his heart he felt a serpent's coil. When night had fallen he ordered his royal barge, and in the mist and the moonlight he sailed down stream. The mist cleared as they went. The King sat in the stern, with eyes fixed far in front; the deep, rapid river drew them onward, and vast trees seen vaguely on either side rustled their leaves in the night-wind or clashed their branches mournfully. The heart of the King rose within him, but no one spoke in the barge, and the tense silence pulsed, as the King Immortal, Lord Royal of the Golden Isles, went forth under moon and stars to find his soul.

The Guidance of a Ring

They came to the open sea. The King stepped from the barge on the fine sand of the shore; he directed his oarsmen to wait and walked some distance from the river along the beach. The keen night-wind blew in from the sea, white waves came rolling in; but he found no Golden Staircase going up to the Court of Stars. The dark hours passed in his dream, the early morning kindled its pallid fire in the farthest East, and the King Immortal, penetrated by the cold and awed by the sea-voices, turned in thought towards the barge. There was sorrow at the heart of all which spoke or moved about him, and the ache in his own heart was like pangs of hunger.

But all roads lead in the end to Faërie, or it is part of the law that a quest pursued therein is ever on the road that leads. As he turned towards the river's mouth, a young man of tall and noble aspect approached and said: "O King, live for ever. Your oarsmen sleep in the barge, and there is that to be done hereby which is reserved for him who is worthy."

The King Immortal looked at the speaker and something

of the zeal of boyhood began to move in his heart. He turned and followed the youth without answering, but deep in thought he was asking himself as he went: "Who is this messenger and what is the message he brings? Is it he who was called by Prince Starbeam a Beloved Kinsman and Brother?" It came to him also that albeit a Magic Ring may insure to the owner perpetual youth and beauty—if these be his—it does not prevent him from growing old in the heart, and that in proportion as youth is preserved longer in the outward body, it may be exhausted sooner in the man within. He asked himself also: "Is this a law in Nature or a rule in Magic?"

Grace of a House in Faërie

The King's Guide directed his course for, it might be, a mile inland till they came to a lichen-crusted stone lodge, older than the trees of the woodland. As they approached it together, a refreshing sense of rest unbound the senses of the monarch. When they paused under the eaves, it seemed all at once of great extent and height. The King said unto himself: "Who cometh from the Court of Stars?" And looking in the eyes of his companion he beheld that light which is to be seen in a Magic Mirror when it reflects a beautiful soul.

He sighed deeply as the Guide opened the door, but that which they entered was like the Sanctuary of a Great Temple. The King Immortal said, and it was still as if speaking to himself: "What must I do to find my soul?"

The youth took him by the hand and answered, as they ascended the Altar-steps: "Let the soul-seeker sacrifice the false immortality of the Ring." And the monarch laid that stone of strange virtue, which he had worn without understanding and enjoyed without deserving, on the sacred stone of the Altar.

The Price of a Soul in Faërie

"What wilt thou give?" said the Guide, "to receive a soul?"

"The life of my life for its life unto life of all," said he who was Lord Royal and King Immortal.

They went out by another door, and he saw the sun shining brightly, the trees casting long shadows, the deep blue sea in the distance and the high blue sky overhead. He stood with head erect and conscious of a light in his eyes like that which is seen in a Magic Mirror when the high spirit of man is reflected in its crystal depth. The King Immortal had found his soul.

A moment after he was passing alone through the woodland and returned to the barge. It is said in the records that he kept his faith with the Everlasting Stars and their messenger. It came about for this reason that one day a stranger presented himself at the palace. He was tall and lean, his garments were of uncouth fashion and coarse material; his face was dark, pallid and very earnest; his dark eyes radiated with inward fire. He described himself as a traveller from the East and besought audience of the King.

"King Immortal," said the stranger, when the monarch deigned to receive him, "in my travels through the far countries I have met with hidden knowledge and have power of transmission to those who are found worthy. There is in particular one division concerning a Golden Staircase and a way to the Court of Stars; but this is not lightly surrendered to the seeker, whom it is sought to prove first. Here is a Magic Mirror which reflects the soul instead of the body of man: it appears as a sacred flame which is sometimes one of great light. But it happens at times that those who contemplate herein reflect neither light nor flame, and not unto such can I give of my hidden knowledge. Look therefore, O King, in this Mirror and tell me that which thou seest."

"Master," said the King Immortal, as he came down from his high state, "well indeed do I know thee."

The stranger smiled and answered, pointing with his lean hand to the Mirror: "Know also thyself, O King."

The Secret of the King

The Lord Royal of the Golden Isles looked in the glass of vision and beheld his soul. When he raised his eyes from the glass, he was alone in a lonely place; the light about him was like a new Eos in Faërie; and his left foot forward stood upon the first step of a Golden Staircase going up into heaven.

The souls are everywhere and ever the souls pass on, they and their life within

XIX

THE DREAM TOWER

The eye of the morning in Faërie led Prince Starbeam ›rth. There were voices which came from the mountains, ·ith tidings from far away and sweet breathings of the ›irit. He found a path over waters and passed the Golden traits to the great mainland beyond the Golden Isles, world of many kingdoms, some on the borders of Faërie nd some of them far removed. How he was carried is :ft to dreamer's choice, because there are many legends of ıring in these regions. There were some that travelled y ferry and some in a moon-shaped boat, but there were lso ships that sailed upon those waters and were not sailed ›y men. There is in fine one story of a ship from a World ›f Stars; but it is not said that it anchored in any harbour ›uilt along earthly coasts. Of other voyage and venture here is not need to speak: it is known that the Golden sles had merchants on land and sea.

Morning Glory of Stars

There is the tale of a milk-white horse which he rode ›eyond the straits, where the bindweed of Faërie is a star :aught in the morning, and it shines through all the day. Che voice and the star led him, the voice which falls from ı star, and the star which sings in its falling. The shadows ›f leaves wrote on the sward in sunlight their guiding vords, and the colloquy of pattering rain with the wind-ıarp in a solitude conveyed its tidings. Thereafter he :ravelled by foot in the wild ways, and a procession of voices followed. It might have been noon when they :eased, and he stood in a certain garden, by a fountain linging its waters high. About this fountain, as it seemed, for ever and ever there hovered a wandering voice, now in the lucent pool from which the pillar of water rose through night and day, now in the stream and spray where the crown of it broke and fell, now in the cups and bells of blooms that starred the turf. The echoes answer in Faërie; they give the word and the message; the secret of all secrets is held in the heart of a song. Of those in their coming and going who heard the Voice of the Fountain there was none that understood. But he, the Son of the Quest, who tarried now in this Haunted Garden, knew well the words and their meaning, that which was told openly and that which was hid in the heart, full of covenants in sunbeams. O storied hills and mountains far away: they told of royal roads and world-old quests of Kingship: like the BOOK OF THE VOICES OF FAËRIE, they told of Throne and Crown; and they told of the Dream Tower.

Words caught and missed

In the old rolls and the parchments there is opened the door which stands between now and then, though not unto all is it given to visit the Haunted Garden and hear its wandering voice. So therefore when he had heard the songs and the stories, all that Psalter of Faërie, Prince Starbeam spoke to the Fountain and said: "My way is long to the Kinghood and long to the Queen of my heart. High Spirit of the Haunted Garden, what must I do to sit on the jewelled throne as a King in Faërie?"

The Voice answered and said: "Beyond the Land of Clouds is a Land of Light. Go to the Dream Tower, which is not reached by him who fares alone. Seek therefore first for one who waits thy coming."

It may happen that the Dream Tower is found at the foot of the Golden Stairs, at certain times in their travellings, for we know that they move from place to place at the will of the Court of Stars: it is known also that the King of the World in Faërie must pass through it on his way. The secret is learned only in the Haunted Garden. So

Prince Starbeam went out of that gramarye, dreaming of houses in lonely woods and grey towers by silent lakes. He walked in a violet light and came, as it seemed to him, or ever the hour of sunset, into a far country, where he beheld presently, all in the great domain through which he passed in his dreaming, as it might be, the doors of a palace, and he on the marble steps. It is to be understood that he did not enter, for there stood one upon the threshold who was like unto a Faithful Companion, a very beautiful stripling, after his own manner and after the eager heart of him.

When they had looked on one another, the Faithful Companion said to Prince Starbeam: "For thy sake and for thy love's sake, I will follow thee wheresoever thou goest." Was this because of the violet light about the visitant or because of his shining eyes? There is something left over in Faërie when all its tales are told: you may ask but do not learn.

Faithful and True in Faërie

Prince Starbeam answered in the glory: "I look for a Kingdom in Faërie, a Crown and Throne therein; but in that path which I travel I must not fare alone."

"I look to the day of thy Kinghood, to be with thee before and after."

Prince Starbeam came out of the violet, and one unto another they gave and one from another they received a kiss of peace. But in this Ritual of Covenant the arms of the Faithful Companion were like those of the Beloved Kinsman, and it seemed to Prince Starbeam for a moment that the lips also were his. He said, after the observance: "Let us go in quest of the Dream Tower."

It was late that summer afternoon when they left the palace behind them and went up a hill thereby. On the summit Prince Starbeam paused and taking up fine sand he cast it into the air. A light breeze rose and bore it to a broad white road, where it fell as a dust of stars. So was their course marked out. The sand is gold in Faërie when it is held by a heart of gold; but gold is sand in Faërie when held by a heart of sand. Prince Starbeam looked once behind, but in place of a palace he saw broad meads and woodland fired as with sunset lights. And the dream in his heart deepened: he walked in the place of a dream, through a world of images. The road wound over dale and hill, till at twilight they came to a weird wooded tract. No breath of wind stirred the inwoven trees on either side of the road. Only a slight rustling sound was heard continuously in the undergrowth. The clouded sunset was dying solemnly in the West, across a stretch of waste land. The twitter of a bird seemed the one sign of life about them. As the mauves and reds faded, they passed again into open country. The town lay a little lower down, an age-old town in Faërie, where lights were shining already through drawn blinds in cottages. The road descending suddenly brought them, as night deepened, where an old one-horse coach stood at the inn-door. There was a green in front and a low bridge beyond. The simple picture wore that aspect in darkness which spoke of great transformations in the light.

Elfin Music at Night-fall

"I have no silver," said Prince Starbeam, "or we might drive to the Dream Tower."

"There are pearls of great price in this sigil," said the Faithful Companion, taking a talisman from his bosom, "and they are stones of many virtues. If we gave it to the coachman he would carry both thee and me."

"Keep thy sigil," said Prince Starbeam, "the night is keen but dry and clear. We can rest when we will by the way."

"Hide it then in thy breast," said the Faithful Companion: "if we travel far I may lose it."

Faërie is Fellowship

The gold and silver in Faërie are silver and gold only in worlds of Faërie: they are leaves or pebbles here. So also the coin of our realms is worthless over there. It is otherwise with stones of virtue, though they keep full virtue seldom on coming out of Faërie. A gem that is worn on the heart and speaks in the heart, filling the heart with gladness, was centred in this sigil. It held the wearer free from fatigue and cold, the fear of darkness and the fever of impatience. Prince Starbeam took the sigil as they crossed over the bridge, and the work of its virtue was like that of a Magic Ring. Looking on the stream and its lapping waves, which lisped intelligible words beneath: "There is health in this water," he said, "and it must be good to dwell thereby. Dost thou feel the happy influence?"

The Faithful Companion smiled, and there came a light in his eyes like pictures of stars in pools, as he answered with low voice: "It is well for me as for thee."

Did it seem like a linking of chains, a promise of life and a promise of joy therein, a giving of love for love? Prince Starbeam said in his thoughts: "Be thou at my side for ever," and then a moment later: "Till the asphodel moves the mountain."

When the village lights were behind them the road seemed dark by contrast. "This cold air is like a river of wine in Faërie," said Prince Starbeam, "and how good is the night and its darkness, glorified by prophet stars." Did the averted weariness and dread of his whole life seem heavy on him who has been called a Faithful Companion, though he is known by other titles.

Heart of Faërie, Heart of Gold

They met presently certain men of strange aspect—as it might be travellers from afar, vicars or emissaries, who hailed them with watchwords of Faërie, and Prince Starbeam made the responsions.

"What are these frightful apparitions?" asked the Faithful Companion, as if one who knows nothing of covenants made in signs, of pass-words or tokens.

Like him who is sure of his journey, Prince Starbeam

answered: "Dost thou not see and hear, my true Companion? They are haunting faces in Faërie and speaking eyes in the darkness, which say that our path is straight."

So they came to a cross-road, and a finger-post pointed the way to the Dream Tower. On the further side of the next hill was another village, where an oil-lamp burned in a little window which was filled with old books, chiefly of Arthur and Perceforest. They went in, and Prince Starbeam said to the Master, as one on an eager quest: "Master, have you any true tales of the Dream Tower?"

"I have none," said the merchant in books, who was a man of tall stature, like a Nuncio of many tidings, full of powers and privileges. "But a stranger passing through the village has sold me, to buy bread in the market, this great folio on THE PLACE AND STATE OF PARADISE, a small quarto on THE SECOND COMING OF OGIER, another—with gold clasps—on THE SCOURING OF THE MORNING STAR, and an old vellum manuscript called THE TURNING OF ANTICHRIST. If you will buy them they are cheap and are worth taking."

"How should we take them," asked Prince Starbeam, "when we are going to the Dream Tower?"

The Cup of Good Fellowship in Faërie

"In that case," said the Master, "step into my parlour and drink, each of you, a cup of wine. I offer this to every traveller who calls here on his way to the Dream Tower. It is a cup of loving-kindness in Faërie and a cup flowing over."

There was another light in his eyes, like a tincture of many sunshines. So they followed him into that parlour, and he served them, as one who pours freely from a flask that is always full. When he had ministered, they saw a pitch-pipe lying on the table, and the Master of the House asked if they would put it to the test; but they had no mastery. Then he himself took it up and played to them, sitting in an old high-backed chair by the fire, while they leaned against a horse-shoe table on which the cups were standing. Sweeter than harp-strings and all our great organs are the far-breathing horns of Faërie. Like voices in the mountains, news from beyond and ever, deep breathings of the spirit, was the mellow voice in the pitch-pipe, telling tales without end, of Launfal and Avalon, of the Earthly Paradise at the back of a Wayside Inn, of the Golden Stairs and the Quest and Crown of Faërie. The voice sounded to Prince Starbeam like that which he heard by the Haunted Fountain. Did it seem to the Faithful Companion as gospel-tidings which come from the Court of Stars, imposing their will on him who is born to be King and on him who shares his path for a night and a day on the morrow? It is neither said nor known.

Change-Ringing in Faërie

When the music had reached—as it might be—the middle way of its unfolding, Prince Starbeam knew and saw that the Master of the House was also that Knight of the Swan who had carried the petition of Faërie to the Great Court of Stars and had come down the Golden Stairs, bringing a Sacred Covenant.

The pageant of sound thereafter produced a pageant of rainbow dyes and a golden broidery of curtains. It seemed that those curtains of music were presently raised or parted and that they stood now in a vast circular chamber. Through stained glass of windows, very strangely painted and imaged, there fell a light which was like the glory of the world, and in such light they beheld Kings of Faërie, from the last even to the first, seated on thrones and with their banners grouped about them. It seemed in fine to Prince Starbeam that they rose up in their majesty to welcome the last inheritor of all their race and royalty, and there was given to him a saluting sign, which they received and again sat down.

The vision changed with the music; they were back in that parlour behind the Book-Room of Faërie, and a voice

The Stars Speak in Faërie

high up in the stars told of the Bright Land lying under a Bright Sky. It is next door to every one, how far and far away.

Prince Starbeam was presently as one standing alone in a place of white marble, and his way-worn garments dropped from about him. He entered a deep well and stood on his feet at the bottom. How cold are thy baths, O Faërie: it was like polar air around him, searching his whole being. He saw moving pictures on the walls of the well, their subjects drawn from the BOOK OF THE VOICES OF FAËRIE, a long succession, one upon another following. The light upon them was like the light of the world's soul. He came forth from that place of cleansing with dry limbs and body. His garments were changed over or taken out of the way, and he put on a nobler vesture. The Master took a basin of chrism and anointed him who should be King on the forehead, the eyes and the mouth, on the hands also and feet, before he was sandalled. Then there came about his head, as it might be, a shining nimbus; and in that same hour and moment he saw the Faithful Companion, like one who has entered a furnace and laid down therein, to be purified with living flame. The rays of it shone through his garments, and each wondered at the great beauty of the other, since this baptism of fire and water.

Again the vision changed, and after all its marvels they saw the Master, sitting in his high-backed chair by the fire and drawing out the last notes of his pitch-pipe. The last note opened like a door quietly into moonlit meadows, and they had passed beyond the threshold, to wit, Prince Starbeam and his Faithful Companion. They were following a narrow path which went up a certain hill. O storied hills and mountains far away: at the hill top they saw through unmeasured distance the lights of a long promontory going out into the sea. In the wind and the moonlight they went down that hill, and they came to the Dream Tower, the place of sleep and vision, the sleep and trance of Faërie. By the watch-posts of Faërie set on its high pinnacles, be it known that they entered therein, *videlicet*, the Dream Tower, its halls and its vestibules, its dimly litten chambers, even to the Bed of Vision. *He giveth Sleep in Faërie*

A still voice said in the ear of Prince Starbeam, so that he only heard: "Take out that sigil from thy heart: it has been thy guide in the darkness and strength in the weary way. Restore it to the Faithful Companion, who has suffered for thy sake."

And this being done to maintain the high seeming, much more did the heart of Prince Starbeam go out to the heart of his peer for this business of the sigil. And it is said that those who have charge unseen in the Dream Tower began to prepare their office. A wind was speaking in chambers and softly in lonely halls, like the roll of years in Faërie, the roll of its ages. It fell away presently into perfect silence, and this was the Presence in the House. Prince Starbeam sat down on the Bed of Vision, and the Faithful Companion prepared to watch beside him, kindling a lamp which stood on a certain tripod. But love is the Key of Heaven and Key also of Faërie, its thrones and its kinghood. It came about therefore that his Faithful Companion was drawn into the arms of Prince Starbeam, who said to him: "Ah, Prince, how I love thee."

And one into another's eyes they looked, as it seemed in the silence, in the very deep enchantment, for a space of half an hour. Eyes in the darkness of Faërie; eyes of understanding; eyes that speak in the darkness; eyes that open the Mysteries; gates of oracles. O the Book of the Eyes in Faërie: Hither, come hither and see. At this long last Prince Starbeam had finished his quest for the Beloved Kinsman and held him now in his arms. *The Praise of Love in Faërie*

But this was the Dream Tower, and the dials and clocks

of Faërie are set to another order than time of life on earth. When they rose up, the lamp on the tripod had burnt itself out long since; it was dark of dark about them; and there came on Prince Starbeam a sense of the passage of years. They went forth into that other night which was outside the Dream Tower, and the Houses of Heaven shone over them. The Beloved Kinsman said: "We have linked up our chain, my brother, in the giving of love for love: it is not long to the Kinghood."

But Prince Starbeam answered, "Blessed is the faith of the Stars and their Covenant under the Rainbow: thy love is my crown and the life of my life in Faërie."

O path of dreams and path of the knowing of dreams: who tells in the morning glory a dream by the light of the moon? What Prince Starbeam and the Beloved Kinsman dreamed in the Dream Tower brought grace of liberation to the King Immortal from the yoke of the Magic Ring. Prince Starbeam said also: "The BOOK OF THE VOICES OF FAËRIE is the Book of Thy Voice. Thou art the speech and the silence. Thy love is a kingdom in Faërie."

A Path of Crowns

The sun came up out of the sea and shone upon the Golden Stairs, going up to heaven behind them. Having taken Prince Starbeam once again in his arms and kissed him, the Beloved Kinsman began there and then his ascent to the Court of Stars. Prince Starbeam looked upward, preparing to follow. His vision of love turned and smiled, raising hands of benediction. In the radiance of that smile the Golden Stairs were taken back into the Mystery of Love.

Love-Knots of many girdles, potent cinctures

XX

THE BELLS OF FAËRIE

Joy-Bells in Faërie

The Bells begin to ring—again and yet again—ringing in the wilderness. Bells of the morning-tide, and light flows over at morning. Curfew at Faërie: does it ring from the Evening Star? Bells that ring up the Moon and Bells of evening dew: Marriage-Bells ringing in Faërie, for me and for you.

The immemorial palace of the King stood on a natural upland platform, looking over the haunted meadows, the downs and sheer precipice. An indrawn hint of enchantment could be felt in the lucent atmosphere when it assumed at certain times a subtle amber tinge, a faint aromatic fragrance, or a wine-like gift of exalting the mental faculties. It was draped in more tangible form by the wealth and bloom of flowers, by the reds and purples of rich vegetation in hollows and high up on holy hills; but perhaps above all by the beauty and sheen of blue clematis, which flourished everywhere, a wild growth of that land beyond the winter. Every flower had its message, a sacrament hiding the grace of some great mystery and thriving in magical earth. O the wild ways of Faërie, lightness and darkness, violet deeps of brightness, and black samite of shadows. The forest on the North lay apart under a screen of gramarye—as it was thought—world without end, or to very end of worlds, because there was no record of crossing it in the old or later annals. For enchantment witness also the wonderful, dreadful moon, an omen and portent, which rose over certain glades and accosted the belated traveller; witness the

The Leaf and the Change in Faërie

strange adventures which befell him and some others; but witness in fine the change of green leaves everywhere as into magian tablets, bearing mystic inscriptions, full of great meaning.

But the precipice, its broad escarpments and the world which opened therefrom were the crowning prodigy and amazement. Far beyond it, in the golden bourne of the West rose the Seven Spires of Faërie—built up at the heart thereof. Vistas between the clouds and paths of light within: between the spires and the precipice there rolled for ever an abysmal sea of cloud—iridescent, splendid, variable—full of billows and vortices, moved by mighty tides. Reflecting every aspect of heaven, it had also inherent light, and it responded solemnly to every wind that crossed it. Now it was white, fleecy and brilliant, now of pearl and opal; again it stretched a smooth illimitable causeway of shimmering grey in a dream beyond the daily dreams of rest.

That which is below is ever as that which is above, and the underworld of Faërie is like the overworld, a place of spells and mysteries. So therefore, when this cloud-sea parted it revealed an infinite depth of azure space, which night peopled with many constellations and sudden bursts of splendour in the appearance of great comets or revolving galaxies. Any high wind of heaven could open frequently in the darkness a long rift from precipice to verge or crosswise; and the cloud-sea, banked up on either side, would be lighted by rainbow radiance of the stellar world below, while ever in the earthly moonlight a broad path of aureated silver seemed calling travellers to seek the shore beyond.

That shore, however, was unattainable; for what boat will bear one over a sea of cloud? The Seven Spires of Faërie scintillated at noon or loomed dimly amidst the incandescence of sunset, an impenetrable mystery. It was chiefly in dream or legend that its winged dwellers crossed the intervening space. But once a day—once in the hour of evening—the Bells of Faërie rang clearly and sweetly. For Bells ring changes in Faërie and their music goes forth in voices, calling over land and sea. There was never a peal of Bells with such sweet voices as those Bells of Faërie. Their silvern chimes summoned the world to listen: many poets, princes and strangers of distinguished appearance came from far places to hear them. When the king sat in his great palace, on that upland platform which fronted the precipice, he too heard them, with unsearchable longing to understand the message of their melody and to enter the world of Faërie. But the desires of the monarch Aureolus—this being a synonym of his name, as it was voiced in the dead language of gramarye—seemed not less remote from attainment than those of his humblest subject. In that region his forefathers had reigned for generations, and each cherished the same ineffectual hope. It was pursued zealously notwithstanding by the reigning son of that royal line, and he held steadfastly to its fulfilment as the master object alike of his life and rule.

Bells of Invocation

This was in days that were spent long ago, when there were many regions of Faërie, many suburbs, outposts and borderlands. Moreover, the task of transmission is to give here and now in the way that it was given of old by a BOOK OF THE ELFIN HOURS, full of strange rumours, resonant with versicles and responsions, a casket of hidden archives from an indrawn world of dream. In the eyes of Aureolus, to forge the missing links and create communication with Faërie would fill the land with splendour and usher in that halcyon age, of which he had heard in old prophecies, which shone ever before him like a flower of light and echoed like melodious diamonds. The welfare of his kingdom was dear to the heart of Aureolus, and he dreamed of attaining by his own enterprise the transformation of his people in the light of Faërie. To this end

A Book of Knowledge in Faërie

he ruled them now, by his justice as with a rod of iron and by his mercy as with a silver wand, till the power of this wise monarch was like a pillar of cloud by day and a pillar of fire by night before the face of the world about him.

From every quarter of his kingdom and from many realms beyond, he gathered knowledge on the subject of Faërie, questioning artists and craftsmen on all means whatsoever of spanning the sea of cloud. He had, moreover, a College of Maidens who divined to him daily in seering cups and crystals concerning things that were passing in Faërie. In fine, there were wise men by whose counsel he erected a great mirror on the highest peak of the precipice, with the hope of reflecting thereon some at least of the enchanted scenes on the opposite shore. But the findings in cups and crystals counterchecked and overcast each other, while the mirror distorted or inverted everything. The King, in his extremity, set up a beacon on the highest escarpment, to burn by day and by night as a signal to the further side. Cressets and fires on mountains were kindled as feasts came round. A ruddy glare in the darkness was cast over the cloud-sea and lent fantastic shapes to tremulous wreaths of vapour. At the sight of them the College of Maidens passed into prophetic trances; they gave visions to villagers, who beheld answering lights upon the Seven Spires of Faërie and shapes of spirits bodied forth in the great sea. But nothing was certain; nothing beyond dispute—save the strength of the king's yearning. And the throne of Faërie was vacant, of which the wise men knew nothing in their wisdom or those who divined to the king in seering cups and crystals.

The Portent of Beacons in Faërie

* * * * *

There is always a forest that stretches, as it is said, for ever and ever. It opens from mystery to mystery, into the middle place of wonders, very secret and still. The desire of the heart is there and the spell of hearts. Of shapes which come out of the wildwood there are tales of enchantment told from time to time, and of things hidden therein. On the skirts of that forest of gramarye, far from the king's palace, a quiet village looked at the sun in the South and seemed to sleep therein. The dreams which came in its sleep were woven about an old legend of music heard in the forest, very sweet and resonant, sounding from far away. The story said that it came from a stringed instrument fixed on a pedestal in a pavilion, and the pedestal bore an inscription which read thus:

Strange Measures of Faërie

Chosen out of all is he
Who knows what means this melody.

The pavilion had a crystal dome and when the beams of the sun and moon fell vertically upon it they penetrated the transparent substance and awoke in the stringed instrument its haunting gift of music. To the winds it gave back no sound; but it was thought that on clear nights the stars shining in the zenith filled it with tremulous vibration. So spoke the tradition; but if one who heard the melody sought to discover the source it ceased midwise in his search, and he was left to get out of the forest labyrinth as best he might. It was transmitted in fine that the Stars in their courses would avenge on him who removed the stringed instrument an affront offered to the Stars. It was protected therefore by the magic of fear as well as by the fear of Magic. The villagers loved the music, and there was a lore of its portents among them; but they did not venture to seek for the hidden source: it was left to the stranger and pilgrim, who failed to find their way.

* * * * *

When the Beloved Kinsman dissolved from view on the stairs by which he ascended, Prince Starbeam remained for a space of moments or hours, apart from all sense of time, as one in a deep contemplation. Thereafter he lifted his hands and prayed for the end of Quest, the day of espousals, the day of Kinghood in Faërie. Betwixt the voice and a silence following after; betwixt elevation and falling of hallowed hands, it came about that he was moving through copse and woodland in the Land of Aureolus, a place of the spirits of trees, the fragrant soul of flowers, the psychic bodies of herbs. Give me the forests of Faërie, the haunted ways therein: their leaves are talismans, the blades of grass are symbols. Give me the music which breathes within the woods: the spirit of Faërie breathes. All its harps are æolian, and there lives no earthly music which is like unto its wind-harps; but in the Land of Aureolus and in the forest on its northern side, within sound of the Bells of Faërie, there was nothing so lofty and blithe as the tones of the stringed instrument.

The Way of the Woods in Faërie

The will of the Stars was leading, the will of the Stars had led. As Prince Starbeam prayed in his heart for the end of Quest, the time of that end drew nigh. The air of a great stillness fell upon the enchanted wood, an expectant stillness rather than one of dream, or a dream as of waking trees, looking for grace to come. There was one more link for the chain, and this was the place of its forging. The earth on the borders of Faërie must share in his triumph, and he must encompass the work which led thereto by the will of the Court of Stars, as preordained by them. To this end and no other was the stringed instrument set up in its hidden place and protected from all comers against the day of fulfilment.

Wisdom of Woods in Faërie

The trees listened and heard that subtle and vibrant stir in the herb-sweet air, or ever the notes began. And Prince Starbeam passed through the forest, as one who goes unawares but straight to the destined place. The heart of the trees is human and so is their voice at times. Wait till the trees of the forest begin to speak in the heart. A secret life pulsates in branch and leaf. He heard the leaves as they whispered: he heard and understood. He knew that he moved on the threshold of strange new things to come. The morning glory of bindweeds shook their bells about him, telling of secret ways and things beyond thought in the forest. He knew not the hour or the day, except that the time of the end stood at his door of life. Without on the downs and the uplands, on pasture rich and green, the Eos of Faërie had changed to glory of noon. O the wild light, the wine light, the wine of the earth and air: they tinctured and scented his way. The wisp light, the gold light through lattice work of leaves wrote words of strange meaning as it filtered through glens and hollows. The air that breathed through lattices was air that brought a message; the message contained a secret; the secret needed a key; but the key was in the heart of the pilgrim.

Power and Glory of Music

On a sudden the first notes of the stringed instrument sounded clear and sweet. A burst of music followed which seemed to fill the woodland, for the path of Prince Starbeam had brought him already very near to the hidden place. There is a soul in the trees of Faërie and a soul in the flowers of Faërie; but this breathed like a spirit which enters within the soul, expanding all its being. The secret of souls shines then upon faces and the heart is an open book. The Herb of Death in the thicket became a Herb of Life; but it seemed to Prince Starbeam, standing tense and still, that his soul was fed by that music with the Herb of Life Everlasting. There was music within music, sweet beyond words in the primary volume of sound, but below this, veiling itself in a deep heart of melodious stillness, was that of another mode and order. It was this which held the message and this which gave it forth, but whether from time immemorial or now rather, in the presence of him who of all was called and chosen, may be dreamed but is not known.

Did he move any longer with earthly feet to reach the appointed place? It is known, but is not said. There is a mystery of coming and going which is hidden in the heart of a rapture. By the star in the heart of Faërie, I know that the Son of the House in the waste and marish chase, having linked up all his chain, and still in the heart of his rapture, stood by the hidden pavilion, under its crystal dome, with the sun at its zenith above. And he who had heard from afar, saw now with his own eyes the stringed instrument, as decreed by the Court of Stars.

What did it tell in the music within and what in the music without? The first was of life in Faërie, and this he heard with the listening ear of soul, for the outward music only spoke to the ears of sense. Hereof are some heads of the telling as the golden moments passed: of visions in Faërie and openings into the heart of vision; the tree of knowledge in Faërie and the tree of life; the tree of death and resurrection and the tree that goes up into Starland; of domes and pinnacles in sunset light; of pinnacles and domes in morning glory; of cities above and below, and of high cities in stars; of the city beyond all cities which is called True of Voice and World without End. But the second music told of the life of quest, the joy of the heart therein, the prize at the end thereof. Of that which remained to be done for winning the Crown of Faërie it also told.

A Chain of Stories in Faërie

At the end of these illuminations Prince Starbeam took up the stringed instrument. With a worshipful heart of devotion and reverent hands, as one who walks in procession when banners are borne before, he carried it through the wood. And whenever it caught the sunbeams the strings responded in music, over and over telling of wonderful ways in Faërie, of secrets hidden in pools and sacred fanes on hills. It came about in this manner that the music heard in the past for very brief spaces only—when the sun stood at the zenith above the crystal dome, or haply a moon in the middle spaces of night—went on for hours and hours, and the rumour spread through the village. Sweeter than harp-strings and all the wind-organs of earth are the far-breathing horns of Faërie; but sweeter than all were the chords of the stringed instrument as it passed through the paths of sunshine from the mid-wise place of the woodland, even to skirt and verge. The rumour spread through the village and far over dale and hill. Now in the sound of waters and now in the heart of a wind, it spread through the borders of Faërie; the leaves in their whispering bore it, and messages fell from radiant clouds—as voices fall from a star. When it reached the palace of the King there was answering speech in the eager heart of Aureolus: he arose and went forth.

Voices of High Proclamation

It came about in this manner that a great procession passed from the court to the village, once asleep in the sunshine and now awake therein. It moved among purple gorges and places of hidden streams. The echo talked to the birds and birds answered the echoes: one theme was blazoned forth. The fruit trees crooned over their fruit, as if they conveyed the secret, and the language of flowers was read no more in the heart but spoken on every side, uttering the same tidings. In fine, there were wandering voices, full of portent and of prophecy, heard among holy hills: watchwords of a coming time echoed in challenge and answer, from peak to peak.

A solitary horn sounded in the high heaven, followed by silence of silence, and even the air of that region one moment ceased to breathe. The procession had paused suddenly, all its paladins, all its priests and princes: those who were carrying censers ceased to swing; and the king's horse stood with hoof uplifted under a stilled canopy, shining with cloth of gold.

A moment only, a space between two moments, and Prince Starbeam came out of the forest holding the stringed instrument, as one clothed in white samite and wearing the radiant nimbus gotten in the House of the Nuncio on the way to the Dream Tower. After such and no less manner does the Court of Stars do honour to those whom it warrants. Of such also is the Coming of Saviours in Faërie.

Beyond the Dreams of Beauty

There are some who have seen all Faërie stand agaze, looking at a glory of glory which had not come out of its world, for Faërie is a dream of Nature and the great visions are beyond. Ask them not now; but they have tasted the sweetness of all life and the sweetness beyond dream. They stood in their high estate, a royal pageant: with a hush in their heart they stood, waiting in amber sunlight. It fell on the stringed instrument, with all blue heaven above: what music over what meadows, what melodies far away; very far away and nearer, nearer and yet nearer; music which sounds at hand, closer than ear to eye—as it might be, music in the heart. While under the trees of the forest the Messenger stood with hallowed hands uplifted and carried all hearts away, the notes of the stringed instrument fell upon the King's ears and spoke to the heart within. A strain of music in Faërie can eat up the years of earth: what did it speak to him who stood in his trance and listened? No one can answer and no one can tell; but the age of the earth went by and the time of life.

The Messenger had the aspect of one who cometh from the Blue Mountains or the foot of the Golden Stairs. As he—the Prince in his coming—stood in the place of vision, a glory within the glory and vision of all was he. The procession broke up and reformed after another manner, congregated in crescent rows at a certain worshipful distance in front of the Bearer. I know not which of them knelt or who stood praying erect with high uplifted hands, but thurifers offered their incense and banners deployed in front, a glitter of golden spangles, a wealth of jewelled stars.

The Dream in the Heart of a Dream

Who has heard in their dreaming that voice which speaks at the corner in a flowering copse of Faërie? A voice unknown which comes like words of consecration, telling of quests pursued, of ends attained in quest and very secret things of an end beyond all ends. The voice of Prince Starbeam was like unto that voice, the words and their sense were his, when the monarch Aureolus came down from his great white horse and drew to the front of the pageant. He came with crossed arms and worshipful head bent down. The Bearer delivered his message, conveyed from the Court of Stars by way of the music produced on the stringed instrument, in the open light of the zenith and rays of the sun at noon. The melody sounded without and spoke to the heart of him who was called and chosen. Aureolus knew in that hour the joy of a term attained, even the master object of all his life and reign: so sweet is the yoke of the law which binds this earth of ours to the other and golden side of the world of images.

And now in a dream of his own making concerning the ends that were his, Prince Starbeam moved forward and passed through the marshalled throng, which rose and divided before him. Thereafter it formed behind and followed the track of the Bearer: but he was led by the spirit and led by the dream within to the upland cliffs and platforms above the sea of cloud. The strains of perfect melody rose and fell in the sunlight, and from time to time in the progress, all among meads and hills, or now in the shadows of trees and by marge of waters, the voice of the High Prince gave forth some part of the meaning in solemn chant—as it were, runes and versicles, maxims of path and term. They are multiplied over and over in annals and secret archives: their name is legion. Those which shall follow hereafter are some in the BOOK OF CONSOLATION and some in the BOOK OF JOY—a few sparks only from the hammering of a great anvil, which gave forth its jewelled fire in streams of light.

I. A thousand years are as one day in the magic of music: the music within the music is beyond the days and the years.

II. All earthly melody seems remembered echoes of what has been heard in Faërie.

III. The desire after Faërie is the desire of a soul for a star.

IV. I have wrought in the wilderness, I have passed through the sown land, I have dwelt in the valley of gardens: there is yet another journey.

V. The head and the heart are thine, O Blessed Land of Faërie.

VI. I have longed for thy ways in the morning and I have found thee in the Evening Star: yesterday, to-day and for ever is written on all thy Gates.

VII. There is no Faërie but Faërie, and it is not there but here.

VIII. The kaleidoscope kingdom of this world is changed in the glass of Faërie, and it becomes another world of wonder: the law is wonder and the root of the law is goodness.

IX. Thou hast given me of thy voices, O Faërie, and I commune with thee in the heart.

X. From over the way, anywhere over the way, out of a great distance, to those who are meant for Faërie, comes Faërie at the appointed hour.

XI. It comes on a white horse, it comes on a brown, in coaches and footwise.

XII. It comes and leads away.

XIII. Paint me thy landscapes, O Faërie: unroll thy canvas for ever. Here is a world to the eye: but we eat fruit of transformation, and lo there is another world—all of thy making.

XIV. From hither to thither for those on the hither side, but further still to go for those who proceed thither—onward and further for ever.

XV. It is always from hither to thither, but the way of the wise is straight.

XVI. Faërie is a great circle and it is far to the centre.

XVII. The world is an outer circle.

XVIII. They are made in each other's likeness.

XIX. The likeness grows greater and greater, the nearer we draw to the centre; for this is the source of both.

XX. O the wild ways of Faërie, lightness and darkness, amber deeps of brightness and violet shadows.

XXI. Glory of grass, glory of leaves, and glory of painted flowers.

XXII. Give me the glory of Faërie till I tire of all the images.

XXIII. Give me the one image, which is love in the heart of all.

XXIV. Give me the last change of perfect being, when I and my image are one.

XXV. The end is like the beginning, and the beginning is like the heart of a pomegranate.

The lilac and lavender of sunset began to tincture the air as the procession arrived at the cliffs and the precipice. Behold a pedestal erected on a highest peak, and Prince Starbeam ascended the steps which led thereto. On the uppermost he paused and turned round, raising the stringed instrument in the sight of all and saying in his lucent tones: "The way into Faërie is a word of sweetness; the path of Faërie is kindness: goodness earns its gifts.

Whosoever would enter shall profess nothing except the works of mercy."

He turned again to the pedestal and deposited that which he bore, when a slant ray of the setting sun fell on the strings obliquely. At the same moment the Bells of Faërie pealed forth in triumph, and the music on either side of the sea of cloud blended in a torrent of melody, building a bridge of harmony which spanned the great gulf. The end had crowned the work. From the peak and behind the pedestal there rose up suddenly the Golden Stairs. Prince Starbeam began to ascend them, but turning on the seventh step he paused with hands uplifted and blessed the kneeling multitude. It is of old and hallowed tradition that the monarch Aureolus knelt in front of all.

The Head of the House in Faërie

Prince Starbeam turned again and went up the Golden Stairs. After this manner he took the Life of Faërie in exchange for the life of earth.

Blessed are the openings beyond the hills, sunset and sunrise, East and West in Faërie, platforms and uplands, height above height ascending, the way of the Path to Heaven

XXI

THE FESTIVAL OF KINGHOOD

The Golden Stairs are ascended step by step for a certain great distance, because it is far to the end of all the golden yokes which bind to this fair world. Thereafter they are travelled in thought, which builds up all our images; but in fine it is a journey in vision through the blue distance, for it is this which leads to the end: the end is seen in a vision: the vision becomes the end. Here is the key of all voyages which are not made in space, and also of paths through stars.

The Flight of a Soul in Dream

But the rainbow's arch is a gateway, and the wonders on the hither side bear no comparison with that which opens beyond. The Golden Stairs end in the golden precincts of the Court of Stars. Prince Starbeam stood in those precincts as one who is present therein and not as one who arrives. If it can be said that there was a portal beyond, it shall be affirmed on the faith of the records that there was a warrant in his heart to enter. He had entered indeed already, for the Court of Stars is a sphere of still reality, and the reality within the soul is not apart therefrom and does not abide without. But here it can be spoken of only within our own world, according to its pageant of symbols, terms of the glory of vastness, terms of meeting and requital. I affirm therefore that the head of the Golden Stairs is a place of marriages, a place of the union of hearts, in virtue of which Prince Starbeam beheld the Beloved Kinsman face to face, in a robe of glory which is more beautiful than the body of Faërie or the astral soul. And one unto another they gave and one from another they received an ecstacy of innermost union which is deeper than anything shewn forth in the state of eye to eye, though indeed it begins therein. The realisation of this union revealed the Beloved Kinsman even to very deeps of essential being, as the Prince was revealed himself in the old and the far time before the beginning of wonders and his election by the Court of Stars. This is true manifestation, but that which takes place when body is revealed to body belongs to the body of things, the state of pictures and veils.

The Lifting of Veils

It came about in this manner that Prince Starbeam knew the Beloved Kinsman as the Sponsor of those who are called by the Court of Stars and the High Spirit of Election. The ground of union between them was the inward capacity for receiving election into his own heart and for shaping all his life to that most sacred end. In so far as the Beloved Kinsman had a human story on earth it was that of Prince Starbeam himself, onward from the time of election; but in this sense it is true that he had many stories, because he was Sponsor of many.

All this is on the side of reality or, as it is said, beyond the veils; but in the bright succession of symbols it is told in the annals that with hands in hands and eyes reading in eyes, as at some of their earthly meetings, they contemplated one within another, and in this act Prince Starbeam was standing presently in the Sanctuary of the Court of Stars, by the steps of the Altar. He looked no longer now on the Beloved Kinsman but on the face of Queen Cynthia, as one prepared like himself for a day of bridal. And it was with him as it was when he knelt at the Haunted Well, so that all which intervened between then and now folded up its scroll within him: it was even as yesterday and to-day when they are taken into a great forever.

The Shewing of a Face in Vision

There are temples that preach, there are voices heard on altars, there are shrined voices in tabernacles; but no elevation of voices is like that which sounded in the minster of the Court of Stars, where spheres gave forth their music, an organ of the everlasting heaven, and Star-Spirits intoned. There are stones that speak in the cities and stones that sing, bearing their faithful witness; but from roof to base the minster was itself melody, and from all its sources the harmony which flowed together was the greeting exchanged between them when the Lover and Beloved met at the Altar Steps. This was the kind of speech and two as one within it.

The Beloved Kinsman was the Usher of the Rite which followed, when priests and hierarchs filled the chancel—even from end to end; and the Miller's Son, first of all in the story who went up the Golden Stairs, carrying his stone of vision, was the leader of acolytes. The King Immortal was the keeper of the Holy Gate, and when there was a battery without, before the marriage began, he admitted Prince Melnor in the weeds of a pilgrim, with staff and scallop shell. He also had been called and came, kneeling in humility and repentance at the far end. The Magic Rings of Prince Starbeam and Queen Cynthia shone upon the High Altar, with a golden cup between them. I testify that the light of their shining was greater than ever it shewed when borne on hands.

A Jewelled Wedding of Faërie

There were those who came from the East and West, kinsmen of the House of Leolyn, princely strangers from lands that are far away, envoys from over the hills, some who appeared unawares in the Waste House when the Ancient Master was committed to earthly rest, and other some who had sent their cause of absence. The Ancient Master sat in a royal stall. There were also many heralds and ambassadors, bearing banners and warrants, and among them those who had exchanged with Prince Starbeam the watchwords of that time on his way to the Queen-Regent and thereafter to the Dream Tower. The

Knight of the Swan, who descended the Golden Stairs on a mission from the Court of Stars in days that were very long ago, came also to this Marriage of Stars, as Seneschal of the Sacred Rite within the Holy Sanctuary. But it is on record that the Daughter of the Stars was about her proper business, because unto her it was given to learn by their own writing, in the prophetic language of the Stars, that Prince Starbeam had other days to follow the days of a throne in Faërie. It is said also that the Queen-Regent of Faërie was keeping the Throne of that Kingdom against all claims and venture till the Coming of the King.

These things are faithful and true; but as annals are silent concerning him, it is to be assumed on our own part that the old Steward of the House had not been called to the Marriage and was well content thereat, because of work in the House and the lamp that was kept burning: it is said of the Golden Isles, on that side of the coast, that it is a place of many shipwrecks. The annals are silent also respecting the Keeper of Precincts who testified once in the past that he went up the Golden Stairs. Who shall say why he was absent, unless he was reading at that time in the BOOK OF THE PROPHECIES OF FAËRIE and hearing answers in oracles?

Hierarchs of the Holy House

The Marriage began, and the Great Presence in the Temple celebrated its Rite of Union. Who knoweth what forms appeared, wearing what robes of glory? But the manifestation of hierarchies above to man in his world below are ever in the guise of man, and it is doubtless for like reason that the Kingship of Faërie became a human Kingship. It is on record, moreover, that the path through humanity is ever the path decreed for all that lives and moves towards higher things. Now Cynthia had dwelt in the precincts, had served in the Courts of the Temple and had been made ready therein, as in a state of still duration, like Prince Starbeam in the Dream Tower. The years that had passed meanwhile in the world of the Golden Isles, the Country beyond the Straits or the Land of Aureolus, were as yesterday slipped through a silence into the now that is, or the space of a rapture between dear lips that join and dearer lips that part. When the Nuncio of the Court of Stars, who once in the past performed a strange ministry on the hither side of the Dream Tower, had put their hands together in the Office of Wedding it was to Prince Starbeam and Cynthia as if she had risen in her beauty out of the Haunted Well at the first shewing of vision. Prince Starbeam made on his knees the Profession of Faërie, a pledge of the King to the kingdom. The kingdom was pledged to the Kinghood, and albeit the royalties of earth are other than those of Faërie and do not lead of themselves to that estate of being, it is said of the Princess Cynthia that she also was anointed and that her covenants were made in his: for womanhood is the soul of Faërie and the heart of all its Magic.

A Chalice of Life in Life

It is certified also that in the last act of this Rite of Union the Magic Rings were dissolved by the Chief Hierophant in that Cup of Wine which stood between them on the Altar. The light of them rayed upward from the Sacred Vessel, which was elevated by his ghostly hands. The starry vintage was administered to the King and Queen of Faërie, on their knees now at the highest of all the steps. O Church of strange adventure: the altars of Faërie are not without their chalices, nor the patens without their bread. Those who are chosen can read in the Missal of Faërie; they can hear good Masses therein and church-bells praising God. But this libation of diamond light, which was drained between the Lover and Beloved, rayed through them, a transfiguring Gift of Stars. After this manner they learned for the first time the use of a Magic Ring; after this manner also was the Solemn Covenant of the Stars fulfilled in a Mystery of Wine. If the astral soul is the body of Faërie, the gift of the Ring received within the body is a spirit which glorifies the soul.

The Rite drew to its close. The King and Queen in their radiance turned with uplifted arms and pronounced on that Blessed Company the valediction of the World of Faërie. It is written that the Kinsmen of the House of Leolyn, the Embassies from far away, the Envoys and Keepers of Mysteries knelt in worship before them. And the Rite of the Temple ended in a trance of its music, as if all the heaven of Stars had joined the sacred choir.

Of ever and ever in Faërie: height and deep therein

XXII

ENTHRONEMENT

The Golden Stairs were taken into the mists of evening or carried up into the lilac distance, away from the earth herself, or else on other service. The multitude rose to its feet, looking towards the Bridge of Harmony and the Land of their Dream beyond. The night fell, the moon rose, a new motion vibrated in the sea of cloud, amidst breathings of buried music. Starry arches, at right angles to the Bridge, sprang momently into being, dissolved and formed again. As if they had lost for a moment their touchstone of distinction between dreaming and waking, the people stood agaze for a space which no one has counted of all the Faërie annalists. In truth there are many records, and some are written in gold, but other some in ink of purple dye. "I have turned them over and over," says one of the later scribes, "seeking the best ending, that I may sing my Compline with you in a good season, with all the anthems and responsions, before I take up staff and scrip."

Hope of the World in Faërie

It is said that the Heralds of Faërie passed over to the Land of Aureolus, bearing warrants and permits; it is said that kings from the earth passed over on white horses to the further side; it is said that the Keepers of Hidden Rites on earth exchanged their watchwords of the time with Guardians of the Gate beyond. I know only that —as it might be—about midnight the monarch Aureolus and some of his College of Maidens, veiled and vested in white, went over the Bridge of Harmony, finding a solid track, and passed beneath the Seven Spires of Faërie.

The doors of a vast hall, midwise in the palace, were opened suddenly in the silence, and within, on that jewelled throne which had stood from time immemorial on a certain hilltop of Faërie, they saw Prince Starbeam wearing the emerald crown and bearing also the sceptre of green malachite, which were his symbols of universal royalty. They saw, moreover, at his side on the same throne, her who was Princess Cynthia, to them unknown as such, and they honoured on their knees the Architect of the Bridge of Harmony which spanned the impassable gulf and joined two worlds together. The King and Queen of Faërie rose in their radiance with uplifted arms, to utter the welcome of Faërie and pronounce its blessing.

A Crown of Days in Faërie

There is offered unto all who read a loving salutation from the Bells of Faërie, and it is testified also that after this manner the desire of the monarch Aureolus was fulfilled in fine. Thereafter on the earthly side of the Bridge of Harmony he dispensed the grace of Faërie. He who by the old chronicles is still called Prince Starbeam full often in fragrant pages—all the Kinghood notwithstanding—had finished his work in the ways without and realised now that the epochs of his past life were like symbolical acts in a great pageant leading up to his bridge-building, that crown of all his tasks, though he foresaw nothing concerning it till the stringed instrument told him its own story and things unrealised belonging to him and his farings. He knew that the burden he bore in the forest clearance was a figurative mystery of his toil in quest, the weird of his ways to come. It was part of the weird that Messengers from the Evening Star should undo at a certain stage the work of the Beloved Kinsman, for the ends of the Court of Stars. He knew also that the Bright Land lying under a Bright Sky is not the Land of Faërie, but a world beyond images, even in a Court of Stars. It is not seen in Faërie: it is heard only, speaking from the

A Land of Life

heart of things. It is over and under and on the back side, but is yet everywhere. It is ante-natal and yet still is native to the soul. It is behind because it has been left and before because it must be found. The Stars prophesy concerning it; they open the way thereto. Prince Starbeam knew in his kinghood the Language of the Stars, like her who was Daughter of the Stars, who read their cypher writing as she read the weirds to come in that other cypher made by the star of the Queen-Regent's kiss, which sealed and shone upon his forehead.

Prince Starbeam knew, moreover, the Mystery of the Magic Ring: to dissolve the outward sign is to find the inward grace. The gifts of the Stars are good, but when they come down it is into the region of mutable things. There is dole in the gem which adorns the outward body; there is life in the gem within: the false immortality of the Ring is the ornament of self-centred being; but it is known that there is another centre, to which in dissolution it brings the draught of life.

The Old House in the waste and marish chase was rebuilt after another manner, and the beacon burns for ever. It is a place of the annals of Faërie and of records of worlds beyond. The Steward of its Mysteries is called by a new name, and the ravaged garden blooms like a precinct of Paradise. It was once a House of the Spirit and those who dwelt therein were a line of spiritual Princes, full of race and royalty; but the old estate had fallen and its history had passed into legend. Some of its archives were therefore like texts written in an unknown tongue. The SWORN BOOK OF THE VOICES OF FAËRIE is really a book of that which works from within: it is of this world on the one side and of Faërie on the other; but the heart of its meaning belongs to the Bright Land under the Bright Sky, which is neither of earth nor heaven. What else shall these transcripts tell you? The motive of Faërie

Glyphs and Hieroglyphs of Faërie

is over all the work: it prevails not only therein but over the whole world, because that which is seen with the eyes of sense and eyes of the astral soul is ever in the world of images.

O World of Faërie, my own country, give me the grace of good adventure: I look to serve a golden cup before the Blessed King. But beyond the world of vision is a world of stillness, and this is the end of all travelling. The power shall not pass from Faërie, nor the kingdom fall away; but after its pinnacles and domes, seen in the morning glory, seen in the sunset light, and after its Mystery of Kinghood, there is another story, and it will be told somewhere surely concerning Prince Starbeam and Princess Cynthia. It is well meanwhile under the Seven Spires of Faërie and in the Land of Aureolus. It is well in the other realms which keep the rule of Faërie: Prince Melnor reigns in one. The tarnished shield of Melnor has been well scoured and hung up; Beryl, the queen of spells, has burned her books of witchcraft and rooted up the false roses from her garden. The horse of the knight Launfal has found his master. The star Lucifer has kindled a new light in heaven; and Antichrist is dead: even Antichrist and Iscariot sleep; their sins and troubles are forgotten. The glory of this world passes away, but not the glory of Faërie. Hereunto therefore is the High Story therein and the Blessed Life thereof.

For the Lion and the Lamb are at peace in Faërie, the Dove is in the Eagle's nest: there are golden waters, rivers of waters of gold, footmarks of enchantment, wings for rainbow flight, and stars following: there is a Spirit of the woods beside me, clothed in green samite, singing through a herb-garden of savours. And this is the very end—I bear my faithful witness—to the Quest of the Golden Stairs and the Way of a Crown in Faërie

PRINTED IN GREAT BRITAIN BY THE WHITEFRIARS PRESS, LTD., LONDON AND TONBRIDGE.

9 780766 107489